MW00878199

IMPOSTER
SYNDROME

EDITED BY

James Everington

&

Dan Howarth

DARK MINDS
PRESS

IMPOSTER SYNDROME

Published by
Dark Minds Press
31 Gristmill Close
Cheltenham
Glos.
GL51 0PZ
Mail@darkmindspress.com

ISBN-13: 978-1974566150
ISBN – 10: 1974566153

This print edition: October 2017

Cover image designed & created by Neil Williams

Edited by James Everington & Dan Howarth

TABLE OF CONTENTS.

Introduction

Dan Howarth & James Everington

You see yourself in the mirror every day, your features and your flaws. Maybe you're happy with what you see, with your strong cheekbones or startling blue eyes. Or maybe you're depressed at the familiar sight of crow's feet, a receding hairline, uneven teeth. But either way, you know what you see is *you.*

We know our own faces and our own bodies; we are familiar with every inch. And they are how other people know us, too; we can only build relationships with friends, loved ones, colleagues because they know us by sight. Likewise, this is how we know them: their faces, their expressions, their physical forms allow us to be sure they are who we think they are.

We are unique and those we love are unique.

But what if that wasn't true?

What if there was another you? Identical in every way. The same strong cheekbones or receding hair, the same blue eyes or uneven teeth. Or what if there was another version of your husband, your wife, of a trusted friend or colleague that you couldn't distinguish from the 'real' one? What if you no longer knew if you were the 'real' you at all?

These are not new fears; stories about doubles and changelings occur in the folklore of civilisations as varied as the Vikings and the Egyptians, while the phenomenon existed in British and Northern

European tales long before the German word 'doppelgänger' began to pervade our vernacular. Literary treatments of the theme range from Goethe, through Dostoyevsky to Saramago; while in the cinema the adaptation of *The Prestige* and multiple incarnations of Jack Finney's *The Body Snatchers* keep these old stories fresh.

And no wonder these stories still seem relevant, in our contemporary world of identity theft, catfishing, and social media fakery.

Ultimately, these stories are about a loss of power. The loss of our ability to be who we are and who we want to be; the loss of our ability to distinguish our associates and loved ones from unknown and possible malevolent others.

In *Imposter Syndrome*, ten authors bring you their tales of what happens when the face in the mirror no longer seems yours alone, or when you can no longer be sure of the reality of those around you. You'll encounter revengeful doubles, twisted realities, siblings of questionable heritage, imposters of all types. You'll maybe spot doublings and echoes between the stories themselves.

Of course, the phrase 'imposter syndrome' has another meaning: the feeling among writers and creatives that they are faking it, that they have no talent, that they don't belong. We don't know if any of the writers in this book suffer from this (though we can confirm at least one of the editors does...) but based on the quality of the stories here, they surely don't need to. They might have been replaced by pod-people, clones, or evil doppelgängers, but our writers are still the real deal.

I Know What They Look Like

Gary McMahon

It was a slow night, but Tuesdays were always like that. The weekend crowds were at home saving their money for the next binge-drinking session and things didn't start gearing up in the city's bars and restaurants until Thursday evening. This was the middle ground: the midweek lull.

I was cruising along Riverside Road, the dark waters to my left and the expensive riverside apartments to my right. I was hoping to pick up some passing trade—somebody on their way home after a late shift or a date or a visit to a friend's place—but for the past twenty minutes all I'd been doing was driving around. No bookings had come in since the old lady who wanted to go to the airport. I was bored. Not even the local radio could keep me focused.

I didn't see the man until I'd already driven past him. He was standing at the kerb, one arm raised. He was wearing a neat black suit and his hair was slicked down across his scalp. I braked slowly, indicated, and did a U-turn so that I could double back and pick him up.

Pulling up beside him, I glanced in my rear-view mirror as he climbed inside. He didn't say anything so I waited until he was seated and asked "Where to, boss?"

He blinked slowly, as if he were waking from a deep slumber, licked his lips, and tried to smile. I say

9

tried to because it didn't quite work. "Do you…ah, do you know the Gables?"

I nodded. "Do you have a specific address? I'm not sure I like the idea of coasting around in that area at this time of night."

"The big tower block as you go into the estate. Dudley House. It's a second floor flat. I can direct you if you're not sure."

I pulled away from the kerb and headed east, towards one of the roughest parts of the city. A police car followed me for half a mile before turning off into a McDonald's car park. A group of four or five men ran out into the road in front of me as I slowed for a red light. The city moved and breathed in its own rhythm. It was comforting, familiar.

I took quick glances at the man in the rear-view mirror. He sat staring straight ahead, which was unusual. Most people, when you drive them somewhere, will look out of the side window, watching the streets move by. This one, though, wasn't interested in the scenery.

Also absent was the casual chatter: "been busy tonight?", or "what time does your shift finish?" The usual inanities mouthed by folk who don't feel comfortable with a silence between them and the driver. I can take it or leave it. If they want to talk, I'll talk. If they want me to keep my mouth shut I'll do that too. They're the ones paying.

I wasn't sure why I hadn't noticed it before, but this man looked familiar. It took me a little longer to understand why, perhaps because it was such an odd thing, but the realisation, when it hit me, was almost physical.

This fare, this man, he looked just like me. He had lighter hair—mine is black, his was brown—and whereas my eyes are dark his were dishwater blue. Other than those details, though, he was my double.

The same weak chin and long nose; the same saggy cheeks and smooth forehead; the same widow's-peak hairline.

I didn't say anything about it, not then. How does one bring up such a topic of conversation anyway? I just sat there and drove, feeling uncomfortable and wanting to get where we were going as fast as I could so I could remove this stranger-with-my-face from my vehicle and get on with my life. As I drove, I was intensely aware of his gaze as he stared at the back of my head. My neck felt warm; growing hotter as I ate up the miles towards his destination. I noticed then that his skin displayed a light sheen, as if his face was damp or sweating.

It didn't take long to reach Dudley House. The tower block stood against the skyline like a sentinel. I'd always hated the place. To me, it represented a certain level of moral degradation; it was a beacon for society's malcontents.

"Thank you," said the man as I pulled up at the side of the road, parking at the kerb. "Could I ask you to just sit here for a little while? I'll pay you, of course. Just keep the meter running."

I nodded at him in the mirror. For a brief moment—almost too brief to make sense—it looked as if he wasn't there; the back seat was empty. Then reality reasserted itself and he nodded back at me, his thin mouth unsmiling. "I won't keep you long." His eyes were dull; they didn't seem to reflect the light.

Glancing back towards the tower, I saw a group of people leaving the main entrance. They were dressed in the street uniform of sports gear and ostentatious gold jewellery. They laughed and clung to each other as they walked, making a lot of noise and acting as if they didn't care who they disturbed. The lights of the tower block guided them; it was their sanctuary. My hands tightened on the steering

11

wheel and I was gripped by a surge of unfocused anger—a sort of rage against everything that was out of my control.

"My daughter is fifteen years old." His voice, from the back seat, reminded me that I was not alone. "Six months ago, she left the house for good. My wife died last year. Cancer. I'd been struggling to cope with a teenage daughter. Katie—my girl—she was a lot to handle, especially after her mother died."

He paused, and I stared out at the sodium-flecked darkness. Despite the car windows being closed, I could hear the muted rhythmic thud of bass-heavy music, dogs barking, a motorbike engine revving in the distance.

"She was using drugs. I knew that, but for some reason I wasn't able to speak to her about it. We grew apart. She thought of me as a joke, a sad old man who was out of touch with the world. She left me for her drug dealer. He has a place here, on the second floor. She stays there with him now, exchanging her body for drugs, helping him sell his product, organising some of the other girls who work for him."

In the rear-view mirror, I could see that his face remained stiff and unresponsive, like a mask. Only his mouth moved as he told me his sad tale.

"I started coming here when I found out where she was. I would drive my car here and just sit inside, watching. Sometimes I'd see her coming and going, usually with him—that man. I don't even know his name. To me, he's a devil."

Passing car headlights lit up the interior of the car, but he remained in shadow.

"She knew I was watching a long time before she actually confronted me. She laughed in my face, called me all kinds of terrible names. She'd become…something different. No longer my daughter, she was a devil, like him. Like the man who'd taken her away from me."

I had the impression that he wanted me to say something, to respond in some way to what he was telling me but I couldn't think of anything to say.

"A few nights ago I finally followed her inside. They were waiting for me. Him, her dealer, and another man with a gun. They shot me in the head when I tried to drag her away. They were laughing. They stood and watched me bleed out on the floor."

He dipped his head, looking down into his lap and displaying his scalp. The hair just above his forehead was messy; it looked thick and coated in something sticky. Calmly, he raised his hand, extended his index finger, and started to scratch at the area. The finger slipped into a hole, disappearing up to the second knuckle. He wriggled it around, and then removed it. The finger came out red, but it looked black in the dimness of the car.

"They shot me and watched me die. Then they dumped my body in the river."

When he raised his head again he was smiling, but it was a horrible expression. There was nothing behind that smile, just a great void into which everything he had ever known had fallen, was still falling.

In his other hand, he was clutching a small handgun. It looked like something out of a film; a prop.

I couldn't move, so I just sat there, watching him in the rear-view mirror. I suppose I could have turned round, but I didn't want to draw his attention to me. He was looking at the gun.

"So tonight I've brought this. But I don't think I'm up to the task."

He raised the gun, and for a moment I thought he was going to shoot me in the back of the head. But he

13

didn't; he slid the barrel of the gun between his lips, into his mouth. He was still smiling, but this time it was around cold steel.

He pulled the trigger before I had the chance to react. The sound of the gun going off was surprisingly quiet: a dull thud rather than a loud action-movie explosion. I saw his cheeks puff outwards from the force of the detonation, as if he were blowing them full of air. Dark blood spattered against the rear window, making a sound like rain.

Finally I was able to act. I opened the door, got out of the car, and went around to the back of the car, tugging open the rear passenger door. The man with my face climbed out of the car. Smoke bled from between his open lips. He set the gun down on the back seat and started to walk away, brushing against me as he went by. A chill shuddered through me, causing me to draw back from him. I leaned back against the car and watched him as he strolled off along the street, the darkness swallowing him. I kept watching until there was nothing else to see.

I got back into the car and drove down to the river. I walked right up to the shore and threw the gun into the black water. It didn't make a sound, not even when it hit the surface. Not even the tiniest of splashes.

My shift wasn't finished but I was, at least for the night. I needed to process everything I'd experienced—the man with my face, the story about his daughter, his faux suicide on the back seat of my taxi. None of it made any sense, not if I thought about it directly. Perhaps if I approached it at an angle things might seem clearer.

I got into the car and switched off the meter, then went home.

Back at my flat, I put on some music and poured myself a double whisky. It was cheap stuff, but it did the job. I couldn't afford anything better than supermarket brand liquor.

The television was on but I kept the volume muted. It was always on. I didn't like to switch it off, even when I was away. On the surface level, it gave the illusion that someone was home. I didn't live in the best of areas—you could see the daunting presence of Dudley House from my living room window—and if people thought the flat was occupied at night they might think twice about breaking in. I didn't have a lot to steal, but what little I did own meant something to me.

Sitting down on my battered charity-shop sofa, I sipped the whisky and pictured the man with my face. Had he really looked *exactly* like me? Now, with the benefit of hindsight, I thought that he'd maybe just resembled me. I was always jumping to conclusions. Jumping the gun. It was a big problem of mine.

One of the lamps flickered; the bulb must be failing. I had a drawer filled with bulbs so the light would never go out for good.

The flickering stopped. There was life in the old bulb yet.

Why had that man got into my taxi? Of all drivers and all the cars in the city, why had he chosen mine? It felt as if there must be a reason. Everything happened for a reason. There was no such thing as coincidence. I believed that with all of my heart. All the strands of the world are connected, like electrical fibres, running beneath the lives we lead. One thing leads to another and then to another; everything happens because of something else happening.

The man with my face had chosen me for a reason.

Of course he had. I didn't doubt that for a second.

Sleep came easily that night, which was a rare blessing. I'd been suffering from insomnia for a long time, grabbing short naps between dreams of screaming faces, burning children and laughing old ladies. I had no idea of the origin of this nightmare imagery, but it had plagued me for years.

The next day I rose before noon, and went through my latest exercise regime. A tight body; a tight mind. The two were connected, just like everything else. If I could keep my muscles hard and train my heart to be strong, the pollution of society could not touch me. It could not touch me.

I trained hard that morning, pushing myself beyond the usual limits. Press-ups, sit-ups, pull-ups using the metal bar I'd screwed into the door frame. Star-jumps, burpees, mountain-climbers. Some karate moves I'd seen on a DVD I got from the charity shop—kicks and punches, lunges and stretches and hard, fast chops with the side of my hand.

It could not touch me.

Breakfast was a raw egg in milk. I'd seen it in a *Rocky* film, and if it was good enough for Stallone it was more than good enough for me. I didn't like the taste but I knew it was doing me good.

On a whim, I shaved my head, using a Bic razor to remove my hair so that I looked different from before. I wasn't sure why this was important, but I felt it was. Some differentiation was needed, between myself and the man with my face.

The rest of the day was spent reading. I'd checked out a book on the Nazis from the local library. It wasn't a pleasant read, but it was a necessary one. Things like the Third Reich and the Holocaust could not be forgotten; they must be remembered, and studied, even by the common man. Lessons must always be learned.

Before I knew it, the time had come to go back out in the taxi. I worked the late and night shifts as much as I could. It fit in with my awful sleep pattern, and for some reason my mind always seemed more agile and alert after dark.

When I left the flat, there was a group of youths on the corner of the street. They were kicking a scuffed leather football against a garage wall and smoking limp cigarettes. I watched them closely as I walked to the kerb, trying to pierce them with my gaze. I'd once read a book about urban survival, and it had recommended a hard, unwavering gaze as a good tool to have in one's armoury.

I rubbed my newly bald head with the palm of my hand and got in the car. The youths stared at me as I drove away, but I held their gaze, even when they laughed and started making abusive hand signs. I just stared and stared at them, not giving any ground—not even an inch.

When I popped open the glove compartment to take out the packet of mints I kept there, my hand closed around the gun. I pulled up at a red light and glanced towards the glove compartment. The gun was there, it was real. It wasn't wet from the river. It was dry. And clean.

The gun had been returned to me.

In that moment, I felt as if a baton had been passed. There came with it a sense of obligation, of duty. By telling me his story, the man with my face had gifted it to me, making it my own story. It was a difficult concept to process, but the ownership of the events that had ended his life had been transferred to me, whether I liked it or not.

All the books I had read, the films and documentaries I had watched, had led me to this moment. They had been preparation, training, so that I might carry out this mission—one for which I had

17

been chosen. It felt right, like some eternal truth that had been uncovered and revealed to me in all its faded glory.

The man's daughter—Katie. I had to save her. This was what he wanted me to do. There was nothing to consider here, no decision to be made. I accepted the task without question. What right did I have to turn down such a monumental responsibility? I was purely the vessel for this man's vengeance, the weapon he had pointed in the direction of Dudley House.

After years of aimless preparation, it was time for me to act.

A giggling young couple approached the car, leaning against each other as they walked along the footpath. The man opened the passenger door and poked his head inside. "Can you take us into town, mate? Club Ritzy?"

I knew the place. It was yet another cesspool, a place where the denizens of Dudley House, and others like them, sold their drugs and their bodies and whatever else they might possess that was worth anything.

"Sure. No problem."

They climbed into the back of the car and I drove away, hitting the button on the meter to start the fare.

The couple whispered and giggled on the back seat, unaware that less than twenty-four hours before a saintly man had sprayed his blood there—blood that had sunk deep into the upholstery, leaving no mark. Surely this was merely another sign of his divination?

When we reached the club, the man paid me—tipping heavily—and the couple got out, staggering across to the entrance. They didn't look the type to be in there. I guessed that they were slumming it, brushing up against the scummy backwaters of the social pond for fun. Some people were like that: they enjoyed the thrill of being close to danger without actually experiencing it.

I sat in the car and watched them come and go: the druggies and drinkers, the sozzled party-goers and the other ones—those that skulked in the shadows and kept their eyes on the crowd, looking for the cracks that might allow them to get inside.

I began to see that some of them had my face.

I'd never noticed it before, but the revelation came as no surprise. After last night's incident, my eyes had been opened to another level of depravity, and it liked to wear the face of those who opposed it. A weak disguise; a poor method of blending in. Like all wild animals, this feral presence had no real intelligence, just a sort of back-street cunning. But I had seen through it all—I was the only one to see.

I could see it all.

And it would not touch me.

A tight body; a tight mind.

I was a man on a mission.

Pulling away, I drove the car to Dudley House. The streets were quiet; the shadows kept their distance. The sickly city lights bounced off the car, deflected by my sense of purpose. This was what I had been waiting for without even knowing. This was the thing for which I had been born. God's lonely man was alone no more; the gun in the glove compartment was all the company I needed.

Dudley House was quiet, too. I could hear no distant music, no barking dogs, and no raised voices. The silence was a doorway into which I could walk, an entrance that had opened up only for me. I watched the front of the building, cradling the gun against my belly. It was warm, like flesh. I felt the heat travelling through my body and into my heart.

I had no idea what Katie looked like but I knew that I would recognise her.

She would be the only one who didn't have my face.

I waited there for a long time, sitting in the car and watching the building, and then I decided to move.

Getting out of the car, I walked briskly across the road and onto the paved tower block forecourt. The lights were on—every single one of them—but I could see nobody behind the windows, and there was no one around outside.

Entering through the main double doors, I moved towards the dim throat of the stairwell, gun in hand, finger cupped lightly through the trigger guard. I'd never shot a gun in my life, but I knew how to use this one. Just point it at the target and press the trigger. This calm self-confidence was another sign, a signpost telling me that I was on the right path.

Slowly, quietly, I began to climb the concrete stairs. I had no idea what number flat Katie and her dealer used, but I was sure I'd find it. People like that, they leave an imprint. They cannot fade into the background; they are too garish, too present, to remain unnoticed.

I inched up the stairs, keeping the gun pointed in front of me, finger on the trigger. I could now hear voices up above. It was as if my ears had opened up to accept the sound.

As I hit the first floor, I heard a door open around the bend of the landing. Music was playing. Somebody was speaking loudly. The door slammed shut and I heard more raised voices. The volume of the music increased as a stereo was turned up to cover the noise. Then there came a muted scream.

I drifted along the landing to the next flight; my feet barely touched the ground; I was floating, like an angel: an angel of vengeance. Up the next set of stairs, gun in my hand, nerves steady, resolve in place. The music was louder up there.

The second floor was a mess. Doors were open along the landing, and people lounged in the communal space, smoking joints and chatting.

Smoke filled the air, making me gag. I dropped my arm to the side to conceal my weapon.

Nobody accosted me as I made my way along the landing, glancing into every open doorway. Inside, I saw people dancing to the beats of different songs, smoking more drugs, counting money. It was all being done out in the open. These people feared nothing. I saw a fat woman shooting up with a syringe. A skinny black man was masturbating in an easy chair; the woman sitting on the floor at his feet was eating a packet of crisps and watching him intently. In another room, a small child in a dirty nappy was playing with what looked like a dead kitten—or perhaps it was just a stuffed toy.

Then Katie walked right into me. She stepped from an open doorway and collided with me. She was short, pretty, with long blonde hair and wide blue eyes. Her bare arms were too thin and covered with bruises. She had on a vest top, cut-off denim shorts, and flip-flops.

"Hey," she said, and I knew in that instant that I loved her. Like a father.

"Come with me. Come with me now." I raised the gun. Her eyes widened even further. Her mouth opened and she tried to speak, but no words came out.

I grabbed one of her bruised arms and started to drag her along the landing, back the way I'd come. Behind us, a deep voice boomed: "Hey, bitch. What's happenin'?"

Slowly, I turned around and shot the tall, fat man who was standing outside the door through which Katie had emerged. Point and press. Like a video game.

It happened in a weird kind of jerky, speeded-up motion. He was holding up a hand; a weak little wave. Three of his fingers dissolved in a cloud of red. He looked like me.

I fired again, and this time I hit him in the elbow. The bone shattered: I saw it all, again in hideously distorted time. White bone fragments flew, blood bloomed like powder. He fell back against the door frame and I pushed Katie in front of me, urging her onward. We reached the stairs. Another gun boomed and I felt my right leg give, at the knee. I swivelled, fired, and the man I'd already hit two times before toppled backwards, a large gun in his hand, his face—*my* face—splitting above the nose.

I limped forward, pushing Katie. She was screaming, but at this point she was still allowing herself to be moved. I bundled her down the stairs. Another man appeared at the bottom, holding a large kitchen knife. He had my face too. I shot him in the throat and he clutched at the wound with a thin, pale hand; blood flowered between his fingers as he went down onto his knees. As we passed him there, I shot him again at close range in the top of the head and his lower jaw unhinged, spraying blood.

When we reached the ground floor, a hand grabbed my shoulder from behind and I felt a hot, sharp pain in my side, as if I'd been punched. I turned, flailing, and saw a knife handle sticking out of my side. The man behind me was short, with a big Afro hair-do on top of a face identical to my own. He was wearing a tight t-shirt that showed off his lean muscles. This was Katie's dealer, her pimp, her boyfriend. I raised the gun to his face and pulled the trigger. Point and press.

His left cheek exploded, giving me a glimpse of clenched teeth beneath the flayed skin. I fired again and his ear vaporised, leaving a ragged hole in the side of his head. He toppled sideways and I pulled the trigger a third time. He was trying to grab the gun in my hand. Most of his fingers went and his chin detonated, coming apart like a badly-assembled toy. He slid to the floor, his expensive trainers skidding in his own blood.

Katie was standing there, screaming. She was pulling her own hair. I tried to reach her but she was already gone, so I did what they always did in the movies: I slapped her across the face. She continued to scream, and then punched me in the face. My legs buckled; I saw stars flaring before my eyes.

Katie ran for the main doors.

I followed her outside and somehow managed to catch her and force her into the car. She was screaming and struggled so I punched her hard in the side of the head. That quietened her down, but I know it wouldn't be for long. I jumped in and started the engine. Figures were running out of Dudley House in pursuit. Each one of them looked for me through my own eyes. I opened the driver's side window and took pot shots at them.

Two men went down; the others scattered. Some of them were holding knives; a couple of them had big guns.

I drove as fast as I could towards the river, hoping that they would be too afraid to follow us. I couldn't hear any vehicles behind us, and every time I looked the road was clear. When we reached the river, I got out of the car and limped to the edge. Pulling back my arm, I said a silent nonsense prayer, and then I threw the gun as far as I could across the water.

He rose slowly out of the river in the exact spot where the gun landed. He was wearing a black suit, white shirt, and a skinny black tie. He took long, lunging steps until he reached where I was standing; then he hauled himself up onto the riverbank.

"I did it...I saved her."

He smiled, and just as before it was an empty expression, a glimpse into the space behind his face—behind my own face, which he still wore.

He moved past me, to the car, and opened the door. Then he dragged her out.

"Please," she said, exhausted. She looked at me, into my eyes, and I could see that she was terrified. "You don't know what he did...the reason I ran away. What he'll do now that he has me back again."

His hands looked huge holding onto her thin, abraded arms as she tried to resist.

As I stood there, confused, he calmly dragged her towards the river's edge. She stopped struggling and hung her head, accepting her fate. He picked her up in his arms and carried her into the water. He did not look back. I kept watching until they'd both vanished beneath the dark surface.

It would be light soon and the police must already have arrived at the scene of my crimes. I'd been dimly aware of sirens approaching the area as I watched the man with my face reclaim his daughter.

When I got back into the car, I checked the glove compartment. The gun was there again. It would always return, no matter how far I threw it, or how far I buried it. The gun was mine now: either I owned the gun or the gun owned me, I didn't care either way.

My hands were wet; my clothes were soaking.

I had no memory of going into the river, but perhaps I had followed them, and then they had sent me away. They could not allow me to follow wherever it was they had gone. There was work to be done. My injuries would heal. Tight body; tight mind. I was indestructible, a rogue cog in the infinite machine.

Shivering, I set off, got back on the road, and slowly cruised the city streets, waiting for dawn. Always on the lookout, hoping that I would pick up another one: a man—or perhaps a woman this time—with whom I shared a face. They would tell me where to go and what I must do; and I would follow their orders without question.

I glanced at my reflection in the mirror but there was nobody there. There was never anybody there. Not since the day I was born.

I kept driving.

In The Marrow

Laura Mauro

They went up to the lough after school as they always did. It might be lashing with rain or blowing up a gale but still they'd go, because they'd done it since they were eight and now, with adolescence heavy upon them and secondary school looming, it seemed especially important that they preserve these little rituals. This part of the lough was quiet, unfrequented by hikers and tourists, placid waters reflecting back the crisp March sky in perfect detail.

Tara sat on the dew-wet grass while Hazel methodically checked each of their traps for signs of activity. When they were younger, they'd half-jokingly set them as proof that faeries lived in the woods; smuggling useful objects from home under their jackets and in their schoolbags, rigging tripwires out of twine and alarms out of baked bean cans on string. Later, when faery talk seemed childish, they'd claimed they were protecting the sanctity of their spot; Hazel had suggested they hammer nails into a board and half-bury it in the mud, but Tara had vetoed that idea straight away. What if they forgot where they'd hidden it and stepped on it themselves? How would they explain that to their mam?

It hadn't been her real reason. Intentionally wounding someone for accidentally stumbling upon their sanctuary seemed spiteful. She didn't dare voice that thought; Hazel would've been disappointed, would've told her she was going soft, and Tara was aware already of the slowly widening gulf between them; the shifting sands of puberty and the sudden desire for privacy, to mark themselves out as

26

individuals, each occupying their own space within the universe: not *the twins* or *the Madigan girls* but as Hazel and Tara. And yet in spite of all of this, they still came to the lough.

"Someone's been here."

Tara turned. Hazel was crouched in the undergrowth adjacent to the dirt path. She held up the severed ends of the thread they'd secured across the gap, a thin reel of white cotton stolen from their mam's sewing box. They'd knotted the ends tightly around the tree trunks on either side to form a makeshift tripwire, too flimsy to do any real harm.

"Must've been the faeries," Tara said, quirking an eyebrow. One hand rummaged in her schoolbag for the tangerine she'd saved. "Quick, get on Facebook. Tell everyone you've proof of the Little People."

Hazel shot her a flat, unimpressed stare. "It's bad luck to talk about them," she said. She opened her fingers, letting the string fall to the ground, a deliberately dramatic motion. "Anyway, you'd have to have scissors to do it that neat."

"Who's going to bring scissors all the way down here?"

"All right, a knife."

"Don't be thick." She unearthed the tangerine from beneath her pencil case, brushed off shreds of eraser with her palm. She realised, with some disappointment, that she wasn't actually hungry.

"You know Eoghan up the lane? He's always got a knife on him, and I bet it's not just him who's got one either. I bet loads of the St. Jarlath's boys carry them."

"But what would they be coming here for?"

Ah, and there was the eye-roll, the release of irritated breath which signalled the end of the conversation. Hazel had always tended towards pompous superiority; the 'older' twin by an all-

27

important twelve minutes, she no longer needed to assert her authority. Her body did it for her. They didn't speak about it; there was still an awkwardness in addressing this strange adolescent metamorphosis, but they both somehow understood the implication. The first period, those strange, subtle changes that meant Hazel now changed clothes strictly and exclusively in private. Milestones that Tara had not yet reached, leaving her in no-man's-land while Hazel strode towards thirteen with a certain cocksure readiness. "You'll grow in your own time," their mam had told her, but Tara wasn't worried. She felt safe cocooned in her flat, featureless girl-body; like she was suspended in time, like she might never change the way Hazel was changing.

She peeled back a flap of tangerine skin with her thumb. The translucent flesh beneath was webbed with white; thick, embossed patches like psoriatic skin. The thought made her vaguely nauseous. She got to her feet, smoothing her dew-damp skirt, and headed towards the shore. Halfway down the gentle slope the grass gave way to a thick rim of loose rock, fragments as big as a fist atop a bed of smaller stones, unsteady beneath her school shoes. Silvery water dispersed gently among glistening pebbles. In this place the shore was so quiet and so far from the road Tara could hear the wind sigh off the water, the rustling chorus of leaves in the breeze. Here, the light emerged piecemeal through a glut of still-bare branches; the sunlight lay in bright fragments on the wet grass, and if she sat for long enough she might begin to feel the first prickling of spring warmth in the roots of her scalp.

"Do you want something to eat?" Hazel's voice was tentative, now; a note of hesitance, a hint of shame at her earlier bluster. "I've got a bag of crisps. You can have them if you want them?"

In the distance, a cluster of blue-painted boats bobbed gently. She watched them dance on the steel-grey tide, timing each exhalation to coincide exactly with the moment the boat reached the top of the swell. "I'm not hungry," Tara said.

"You're never hungry." She heard the rustle of the packet as Hazel opened it, the moment's pause before she began to eat them. "Are you cross with me? Don't be cross."

"No." She turned around. Hazel had spread her coat out on the grass and was sat there, one white sock half-sunk into the heel of her shoe, dark hair lank and heavy about her face. Old paint speckled the collar of her school jumper. In that moment—pale eyes wide and quizzical—she looked almost a child again.

Tara realised then, with some alarm, that the ground was moving. "Hazel," she blurted, reflexive; the grass undulated with the same slow, sinuous motion of the water behind her, and somehow she could feel it underfoot, the displacement of solid ground beneath her shoes: *rise and fall, rise and fall,* a queasy rhythm. "Hazel, something's wrong."

Hazel looked up. "What? What's wrong?"

She tried to formulate a response, but the act of speaking seemed insurmountably challenging; the effort required to open her mouth, to push each word out past her lips. Exhaustion washed over her like the last dregs of a tsunami. Her knees buckled; her body felt suddenly boneless, impossible to manoeuvre, and as Hazel leapt up to catch her, she was grateful for her sister's strong arms, lowering her gently to the ground, and the faraway murmur of her name over and over like waves crashing on a distant shore.

Ⅱ

The hospital smelled all wrong: sharp and astringent, like the antiseptic Mam used when she or Hazel had grazed a knee. The sheets smelled of the wrong type of laundry powder. And there was so much *noise*, all the time, a strange symphony of beeping machinery and hushed conversation, the keyboard clatter of shoes on linoleum. You couldn't hide away here the way you could by the lough; the curtain around her bed was barely enough to obscure the constant traffic of nurses and doctors and worried parents passing back and forth, and it seemed to Tara that if she could see them, they must surely be able to see her too.

She looked down at her arm. A thick weft of cotton wool was taped to the crook of her elbow. The tape hurt to peel off, so she'd given up trying. The nurse had been gentle, and she'd wanted to seem brave, but the needle had stung so badly that a few tears had still escaped her tightly-shut eyelids. Still, the nurse had smiled, and called her a brave girl. Tara thought she was probably a bit too old for that sort of compliment but she took it with grace, because it seemed to make Mam happy.

Mam had gone to get something to eat, and Dad had taken Hazel home hours before. There was something peculiarly lonely about a hospital bed— the not-quite isolation of the drawn curtains, the way every nurse seemed to know who she was, and why she was here. The way they'd smile, all tight and false, when she asked what was wrong with her. Like they were all in on some kind of secret. Hazel did that sometimes, when she was trying to get in with the older girls. All that stage-whispering, the knowing looks passed between one another like a message. Hazel's downfall was that Tara didn't care what the big secret was, and had never made a show of pretending. If a secret could be so life-changingly important it made precious little sense to her that it should be kept in a box and passed back and forth between a select few, the way boys at school might pass round a toad caught in a Tupperware container.

She wondered what Hazel was doing now. She wished, not for the first time, that Mam would make good on her promise to let them both have phones; she knew Hazel would have texted her by now, asking if she was all right and, no doubt, fishing for gory details. Sending her dumb jokes that made sense to nobody else but them; obscure references to a lifetime's worth of in-jokes and mythology. Holding her hand, though they were a few miles apart.

The curtain rustled. A tall nurse stepped through; she had boat-broad shoulders, torso as thick and solid as an oak. There was no false cheer about her; she did not even pretend to smile. "Where's your mum?" she asked.

"She went to get coffee," Tara said. And then, because she was tired of all the secrecy and the not-knowing: "Why won't anyone tell me what's wrong with me?" There was a distinctly childlike whine to her voice; she had tried in vain to shed that whine, to cultivate the bolshy, commanding tone she'd heard Hazel utilise. "When will I be able to go home?"

The nurse looked silently at her for a moment. Tara wondered what she saw: a thin broomstick of a girl, wan moon-face and dark wire-wool hair, all bruised knees and grubby palms. Not a young woman, but a fragile child. She knew this to be true because the nurse visibly softened, touched, apparently, by the fearful petulance of her voice. "We're not sure what's wrong yet," she said. "We need to run a special test to find out."

Tara's brow furrowed. "What sort of test?"

"The doctor thinks that there's something inside your bones that's making you feel poorly. We need to get a special needle and go inside your bones to take a sample of the marrow. It sounds scary, but—"

"I'm not scared," Tara blurted, though even the thought of needles made her faintly queasy. She struggled upright, pulling her lead-heavy limbs into a sitting position. The effort made her head spin a little bit, but she held firm. "It's okay. You can do the test." Thrusting out a skinny arm, already bruised from the phlebotomist's efforts. Her veins were a bright blue roadmap beneath translucent skin. "And then I can go home, can't I?"

The nurse opened her mouth to speak, but paused, hand poised; she pursed her lips, tucked Tara's defiantly outstretched arm back beneath the blanket with unexpected gentleness. "Yes, probably," she said, patting Tara's shoulder gently with one broad hand, and though she was smiling Tara did not miss the sadness in her eyes, brief but definite, like a cloud that momentarily blots out the sun.

II

They did not use the word 'cancer' around her, though Tara knew that was what leukemia was: a cancer of the bone marrow, infiltrating the blood. She was in hospital for two days before they eventually let her go, bruised and depleted and heavy with this new burden; these microscopic invaders swirling sluggishly in her veins, masquerading uselessly as white blood cells, unable to fight infection like they were supposed to. Mam and Dad had stayed with her in shifts. Hazel had been all but forbidden to visit; a hospital, Mam said, was not a good place for a young girl to spend too much time. The irony of Tara's sickbed incarceration did not seem to register.

The sunlight seemed too bright as they stepped out into the car park, the sky a vivid, alien blue like a tarpaulin draped over the curve of the Earth. Tara put one foot in front of the other, steady all the way to the car. She put on her seatbelt, staring out of the window as the hospital receded, as Galway receded. She understood that everything had changed, but somehow nothing felt any different: the car still smelled like wet dog and lemon air freshener, Dad still sang loudly along to Merle Haggard on the radio, and still got the words all wrong. And perhaps Mam looked a little more tired than usual, her skin a little more creased, like she'd got older overnight, but two days carting back and forth between Galway and home would make anyone tired, wouldn't it? Mam looked back at her and smiled—a too-tight smile, full of teeth—and asked if she would like to go to Mr Waffle for lunch, because wasn't Mr Waffle her favourite? Tara shook her head mutely in response; the thought of food held no appeal whatsoever. And she understood then, from the sudden glassy-eyed despair on her mam's face, that everything really had changed.

II

It was the way Hazel shrank away from her as she walked through the door that hurt the most; more than the needles and the blood-pressure cuff like a vice around her bicep, more than the deep, pulsating ache in her hip where they'd pierced the bone and sucked out the marrow. That look of helpless horror on her sister's face; limbs drawn sharply inwards, head tucked into her chest, like she could smell the cancer emanating from Tara and was trying desperately to keep it out of her lungs.

Hazel said nothing as Mam led Tara up the stairs, into her room—*her* room, not *their* room, because they were almost teenagers now, and Dad had partitioned the master bedroom the previous year so that they would have the privacy everyone seemed to believe they would need. Tara sat on the edge of her bed, staring over at the wall; the Adventure Time posters and the half-finished crochet projects trailing pink wool like innards across the desk, the stupid sunflower-yellow paint she'd argued so hard to have and quickly grew to hate. And somewhere on the other side, Hazel's bed; her pared-down décor, all visible traces of childhood purged. If she died, Tara wondered, would they take the partition down so that Hazel might have the whole room to herself? Would she throw out all of Tara's things—scrunching her nose in disdain at her cuddly toys and her glitter pens—or would they leave everything exactly as it was, perfectly preserved, the crease of the bedclothes the last solid proof that Tara had ever existed in corporeal form?

She hadn't cried when the doctor, who had blonde hair pulled in a bun behind her head, had explained to her just how sick she was, when she'd told her she would have to spend a few weeks in hospital while they blasted her body with chemicals to kill off the cancer ('disease', she'd called it, like it was only the flu.) But here, now—bone-tired and sore, stomach like a clenched fist, staring at the paraphernalia of her childhood—she let the fear and the anger and the sharp-edged unreality of the past few days wash over her, a cold black tide closing in over her head. She allowed herself to sink, to yield to the unbearable pressure, an anvil placed directly over her heart, crushing her lungs until it was all she could do to draw in each tearful, gasping breath. It wasn't the realisation that she might be dying that broke her but the way Hazel had recoiled, appalled by her sickness; not the thought of dying, but the thought of dying

34

without her sister by her side. The thought of dying alone.

II

She woke in the middle of the night to the sound of someone else's breathing, the sticky-soled patter of warm feet on floorboards. She peeled her eyelids open, wiping away crust with her knuckles; it felt as though she had been dragged from the most abyssal depths of sleep but that couldn't possibly have been so.

Hazel was a grey silhouette in the light peeking through the curtains; her hair was rumpled and her pyjamas a little askew. She shambled towards the bed; Tara lifted the sheets, an automatic motion, scooting up against the wall to make space for her sister. When they were smaller and shared a bedroom, they would do this all the time; one would creep across the room, into the other's bed, and they would lie side by side, talking very quietly until they inevitably dropped off to sleep. Tara couldn't remember exactly when they'd stopped; it just seemed strange, suddenly, to share such close proximity, though they had never thought much about it as children. Tonight, it felt comforting; her cold bones slowly absorbed the warmth of Hazel's body, and the sound of her breathing reassured Tara that for now at least, she was still alive.

She felt the tickle of Hazel's hair as she turned, shifting her weight; Tara felt strangely flimsy beside her, as though she was only a piece of carefully-folded origami beside Hazel's flesh and bone and substance.

"I know your secret," Hazel whispered.

"Being sick isn't a secret," Tara muttered. Then, for emphasis: "*Cancer* isn't a secret. Mam's already rung school. Everyone will know by now."

Hazel was silent, and anxiety needled at Tara's stomach; she wondered what she'd said to upset her. Was it the C-word, spoken so blatantly? Should she have cushioned it in comfortable euphemisms, made it sound less threatening, less alien?

"I didn't mean that," Hazel said, after a time.

"Then what? I don't have any secrets. I tell you everything. You know that." She stared up at the ceiling, suddenly irritable. She felt bruised all over, her joints like poorly-oiled hinges. She imagined the cancer cells swarming inside her; ugly little blobs consuming and multiplying, heavy in her veins. It seemed very unfair, suddenly, that Hazel should feel uncomfortable with Tara's illness when she was the one being eaten alive. "I don't feel very well, so either stop being a gowl or you can go back to your own bed."

Hazel ought to have apologised, then, as she usually did when Tara snapped. Instead, she slipped wordlessly out of the bed. Tara squeezed her eyes shut, waiting for the sound of feet receding towards the door, the creak of the floorboard in the hall, perhaps the huffy slamming of her door despite the hour. There was nothing.

Her eyes opened. Hazel stood there, very still, staring down at Tara. Her lips were curved slightly upwards, an almost absent half-smile. Distant, as though caught in a blissful daydream. She leaned down until her mouth was level with Tara's face; she could feel Hazel's breath like a warm wind brushing past the coracle of her ear.

"I know you're not really Tara," she whispered.

She left on feather-light feet, almost dancing to the door; pride, Tara realised, and a shiver ran the length of her body. She felt suddenly feverish as she pulled the covers up over her head. A strange, sick sensation boiled in her stomach as she recalled the uncanny smile, the way Hazel had loomed in the dark like a ghost at her bedside. She did not know the meaning of her sister's proclamation, but she knew that Hazel believed, absolutely and without question, that she was right.

Ⅱ

Three days later they admitted Tara to the children's ward. She would spend the next few weeks in hospital, perhaps longer. There were other words, things Tara did not understand but took to be important: something about abnormally low neutrophils and platelets, culminating in a promise that they would be extra careful to avoid exposure to bacteria and viruses. Mam scribbled a list on a notepad of all the things she must avoid eating, although Tara did not feel like eating much more than the occasional slice of toast.

She'd been out of hospital barely even a week before they took her back in. It seemed that every time Tara began to process what was happening to her there was a fresh deluge of information. She cast her arms about, frantically gathering the few snippets she understood before they drifted away from her. She brought a notepad to the hospital, a pencil case: *Here are the facts*, she wrote, because it felt like something she ought to document. Perhaps she could start a blog once she had her thoughts in order. If she ever got them in order. She wrote with felt tips, using a different colour for every numerical point: *1) My name is Tara Marie Madigan. I am twelve years old, thirteen in June. 2) I am sick with lukemia 3) I have a twin sister called Hazel Sian Madigan who is not sick*

37

4) I might die, altho the dr says there is 'every chance you will make a full recovery'. I think the dr is telling lies, because I heard mam crying last night and she hardly ever cries about anything.

Her pen hovered above the page, uncertain.

5) hazel says I am not really tara. I don't understand what she means by

"What're you writing there?"

Tara threw a jealous arm over her notebook. "None of your business," she said, glaring up at Hazel, whose schoolbag was slung over her shoulder. She grinned at Tara like she knew some kind of brilliant secret and did not intend to share it. "Shouldn't Mam and Dad be with you?"

"They went to get coffee."

Hazel dug into her bag, unearthing an exercise book and accompanying novel, which she placed on Tara's bedside table. "What's the point of being off sick if you're just going to do school work?"

"I don't want to fall behind." The smell of wet earth rose, rich and familiar. Tara peered down at Hazel's shoes. The soles were rimmed with thick mud, sprigs of torn-up grass. "Did you go to the lough without me?"

Hazel shrugged. "I had to check the traps," she said. Her eyes briefly appraised Tara's curled-up body: legs pulled up to her skinny bird's chest, the port they'd installed there barely a lump beneath her pyjamas. She peered up at Hazel through the dark wisps of her fringe; was Hazel checking her for changes? Was she assessing the Tara-ness of her appearance?

But that's our place, Tara thought. *We always go together. We always have.* She closed her notebook, recapped the felt pen. "They won't let me outside at all," she said, tilting her head so she could better see

38

Hazel. "Isn't the lough a bit quiet on your own? Does the house feel strange without me there?"

"It feels strange without *Tara* there." Hazel's face was entirely serious now, no ghostly smile or knowing look in the eye. "How long has it been *you*, anyway? Do you even remember? I guess you probably don't, do you?"

Tara sighed. "Hazel, I don't understand a word you're saying. I *am* Tara. I've always been Tara." She paused, biting back her irritation before it could blossom into anger. "You've only been acting this way since I came back from hospital. What, are you scared of me dying? Is that why you're pretending I'm someone else?"

Her nose wrinkled. "Why would I be scared of *you* dying?" she said. Her face contorted; an expression of faint disdain so genuine that a sudden anxiety seized Tara's muscles, a sharp and unpleasant electric shock. She was used to Hazel's moods, her fits of random cruelty—the cat-and-mouse compulsion to wound, to maim, gone almost as quickly as it arrived. This, though; this was not *that.* Tara felt the sincerity of Hazel's words as sharp as a fist to the jaw.

"Who..." The rest of the question seemed stuck in her throat, a solid glut of words lodged somewhere deep. She swallowed hard. "Who do you think I am, Hazel? If I'm not Tara, then who am I?"

The disdain deepened until it looked almost like pity. "You *know* what you are," she said. There was no malice, no aggression. She sounded bored, like this was a game she had grown tired of playing. "They've been setting off all the traps. Even the secret ones I put there, the ones you don't know about. That's how I know they've been watching us."

"*Who?* Who are you talking about?"

39

"The little people," Hazel said. "The *faeries.* I'm not sure exactly when they switched you. It's hard to say. You were very good at being Tara for a while, but you've not been so good at it lately. I *know* my sister. She's always been a bit soft and a bit whiny, but not like you. I knew there was no way Tara could change so much, not in such a short time." Her eyes fixed on Tara's, pale and intense. "You know why you're sick, don't you? It's not leukemia or anything like that. It's because you've been away for too long. Because this isn't your world. It doesn't matter how much medicine they give you. You'll get sicker and sicker and then you'll die."

"You're not serious." It was ridiculous. *Hazel* was ridiculous. And yet when Tara searched her sister's face for some sign of spite, some hint of gleeful, bright-eyed mockery, she saw nothing but smug triumph. The broad, satisfied grin of one who believed they had everything figured out.

"They usually switch people when they're babies. Changeling. That's the word for you. They take the real person back to *their* world and leave something else behind. Sometimes they make you out of wood. Mad, isn't it? A magic lump of wood made to look like a person. And sometimes, they leave one of their own behind. But don't worry." Gentle now, placing a consoling hand on Tara's shoulder. Hazel felt warm, alive; a strong pulse beat in the cup of her palm, an abundance of hot, healthy blood. "I'm going to sort all of this out. I'm going to find Tara and bring her home. And then you can go home too."

But I am home, Tara thought, desperate; she wanted to grab Hazel's stupid fat shoulders, to shake her until her brain rattled in her skull, yell at her full in the face: *I am your sister. I have always been your sister. You can't just imagine me away because*

*you're afraid. You can't just abandon me when I
need you most.*

Instead, she asked: "If I'm a faery, or…or a piece
of magic bloody wood or *whatever* you think I am,
how comes Mam and Dad still think I'm me?"

"Parents always think their kids are perfect,"
Hazel said. "When I find Tara and bring her home,
Mam and Dad won't realise anything's changed.
When Tara gets better, they'll say it's a miracle. I'll
take you down to the lough and you'll go back to
your world, and they'll never know the truth." Her
smile was indulgent. Sharp at the edges. "Sure I'll
know, though."

♊

On her fifth day in hospital Tara spiked a fever.

At first it was mild; her muscles grew taut with
the imaginary cold, breaking out into shivering fits.
She lay depleted and miserable, slipping in and out of
sleep; there was a stack of books on her bedside
table, an iPod with earbuds dangling just out of reach.
She lacked the energy to grab for them; the idea of
focusing on a book for long enough to take any of it
in seemed laughable. She lay, and her body trembled,
and the sweat glued her fringe to her forehead, her
face to the pillow. When she dozed, she dreamed of a
turbulent sea, spray crashing over the side of her tiny
boat; she dreamed that black clouds were gathering,
and that she was sailing straight towards them.

The fire inside of her grew, feeding on the meagre
fuel of her depleted body; dead cells and poisoned
dregs, burning up her flesh as she drifted in and out
of a fitful sleep. It grew increasingly difficult to tell
when she was awake. The world seemed wrong,
somehow; too bright, too colourful. Everyone seemed
blurred at the edges, leaving faint trails when they

moved like dissipating stains. She imagined she could taste it, the essence of everyone who had been near her, everyone who had shared the same air as her, like ash from a crematorium filtering up her nose, into her mouth. She chased the trails with lazy fingers, imagined them sifting between like sand.

There were loud voices. Sharp stings which must have been wasps; if she squinted, she could see them, small and fast against the blue walls. She swatted as they came close, determined that they would not harm her again, but then someone was holding her down, cold hands against her hot skin, whispering words she could only partly understand: *medicine, it's only medicine, you want to get better, don't you?*

If it's medicine, she thought, collapsing back onto her sweat-soaked pillow, *how come it's making everything worse?*

It came to her between dreams, in that grey, liminal space where she was neither asleep nor truly awake. A memory spark, weak and sputtering but there, a small point of clarity in the fever-fog: *sometimes, they make you out of wood. Of course,* she thought, looking down at herself—twig-limbs and stick-girl body, hospital pyjamas like loose, hanging skin. Hazel was mad, but perhaps in that madness there was a truth. Her body was on fire, and fire consumed wood. Fire gobbled wood up and left only ashes.

Struggling, she reached up with one bent-branch arm. The water jug was set high on the bedside table, but she snagged it with her fingers; the minute crackle of bark as she clasped the handle, dragged the plastic jug off the edge. The lid slipped off. Water sloshed from the spout, a great cold gout of it soaking through the thin stuff of her pyjamas. She gasped involuntarily at the sudden chill. Carefully, she poured the rest of the jug over herself, anointing her forehead with it, her belly, her legs. Water to quell the flames. Medicine was for flesh, for blood; she was bark and sap and dry, smouldering wood. She was sure of that now, as sure as she was of anything.

She left the jug empty on the bed beside her. Already the water had begun to evaporate, rising from her hot skin like smoke. Fingernails pried at the uncomfortable protrusion where they had placed the port, anchoring in the skin; if she could just peel off that useless coating, get to the bark beneath, she could douse the embers before the fire sparked back up. Her nails were rough-edged stubs, prying at the plaster, peeling it back; she caught the skin with the edge of a nail, opened up a long, thin rift. Dark blood welled up in the gap. It seemed odd, she thought, that there should be blood there at all. Diligent, she worked at the seam with her fingernails, pulling back the meagre flesh, and *there*, just beneath the skin, the barest glimpse of ragged bark.

"Jesus, Mary and Joseph."

She looked up. Someone was there, watching her; their face drifted in and out of focus, though she could see the whites of their eyes, the dark hole of a wide-open mouth. She lifted her hands. Her thin fingers glistened red. "There's a fire," she said, but her lips felt strange, her voice like treacle in her throat.

"She's burning up," someone else said. They seemed to be standing beside her, though she wasn't sure how they'd got there. "She must be hallucinating."

"Jesus. Hallucinating *what?*"

"Someone get Doctor Conver. Keeley, we need to get this port back in."

The noise washed over her, peaceful, meaning nothing at all. Someone was holding her hands up, examining the tips of her fingers. *The buds are*

43

blooming, she wanted to say. *There'll be blossoms soon.* But the fire was coming back, and the heat of it was making her drowsy. She closed her eyes. In her dreams she was at the lough, and the wind was loud in the trees. Far away, on the other side of the water, someone was calling to her. She raised her arm, wiggling her twig-fingers in greeting, and marvelled at the beautiful red flowers bursting from the tips, bright and glossy in the sunshine.

Ⅱ

She spent more time asleep than awake. Consciousness required an effort she felt barely capable of; she could barely tolerate the constant sourness in her stomach, the taste of bile in the back of her throat no matter how much gum she chewed. Mam and Dad came and went. They would talk to her, read to her; they would feed her miserable little morsels of cake and lemonade, then despair as she brought it all back up again minutes later. She would smile between bouts of desperate retching, reassure them that she was feeling better than she looked, and then she would ask if they could read to her for a bit while she rested her eyes. Sleep came mercifully quick, a black and blissful totality. She did not dream; she simply shut down.

There were discussions with Doctor Conver. She could barely follow them, except to understand that she was not improving as much as they had hoped. Doctor Conver looked like she was Mam's age, a fat, pretty woman with sandy blonde hair and a spattering of freckles; she wore a severe white labcoat over sequinned jumpers, gaudily patterned blouses, necklaces as bright and chunky as Dolly Mixtures. She smiled even when the news was bad, and Tara understood this was not for her benefit—she *knew* how bad things were, she felt it every waking moment—but for Mam and Dad's. It was a small measure of hope, and they clung to it the way a dying man clings to a priest's absolution.

She did not understand the words Doctor Conver used—*her white cells are barely adequate, her platelet count is not improving, we need to do another biopsy to see if the chemo has worked*—but she understood what it meant. She was not getting better. She would not get better; the next infection she contracted would be the last. The fever would burn her to ashes. They continued the chemo anyway, because there was nothing else they could do, and because sometimes, Doctor Conver told her, the most powerful medicine of all was hope.

After a while, it hurt to look at Mam and Dad. The too-gentle way they'd smile at her. The way they'd feed her little questions, fishing desperately for anything they might interpret as good news: *I ate some lunch today. I read a few pages of my homework. I walked to the toilet and back by myself.* She would lay still with her eyes closed, feigning sleep until it overtook her for real. Her fingers would pry at the gauze taped to her chest, covering her wounds; she would press with the pad of her thumb and feel the hard, flat planes of her sternum pushing up beneath her emaciated flesh. *I am a real person*, she told herself, though the hallucination was still vivid in her mind; she could remember, with startling clarity, the way the blood-wet bark had looked in the cleft of her torn skin.

In the end, they let her go home. "We'll bring her back for a biopsy in a few days," Doctor Conver told them. "But for now, it's best for Tara to recuperate in her own environment. She's been through a lot here. It'll be good for her to spend time in familiar surroundings."

The last time she saw her parents—her *flesh* parents, tired and ragged but solid, reassuring, refusing to give up despite her continual failure to improve—she asked if they would read for her. She intended to stay awake this time, though her body was a crudely-stitched patchwork of aches and niggles, and her bed was not as comfortable as she remembered it to be. Mam plucked a book from the shelf. She smiled gently, pink lipsticked mouth and powdered skin, exhausted but still striving for normality.

"I'll read your favourite," Mam said, and lifted the book so she could see the cover: stark, black and white, well-loved and well-thumbed. *Noughts and Crosses.* She knew instantly she had never seen it before. She knew she ought to have. She lay there, fighting to stay awake as Mam read her Tara's favourite story, savouring every word for the first time, and she wondered how it was possible that Hazel could have known everything all along.

♊

She felt Hazel shaking her, pulling her from the warm depths of sleep: "Wake up. It's time to go."

"Time to go where?" She rubbed the back of her eye with one hand. A faint greyish light suffused the room, spilling in through a gap in the curtains; the sky outside was dark still. It was not yet dawn. "Hazel, what time is it?"

"Ssh." A finger pressed to the lips. Hazel was fully clothed; she wore grubby white trainers, her school parka. "You'll wake Mam and Dad. Come on, get dressed. We're going to the lough."

Her bones felt hollow; cracked open and sucked dry, all her marrow turned to dust. It seemed that there was nothing left inside of her but thin, watery blood and the last dregs of poison. "Don't talk shite," she muttered, pressing her face into the pillow. "We're not going anywhere. It's the middle of the night. Let me sleep."

She felt Hazel's hands on her shoulders, gently prying her up off the mattress; she was featherlight, a doll in Hazel's arms. "There's barely anything left of you now," she said, not unkindly. "Come on, now. It's time to go home."

"Home." This had been home once. She looked around the bedroom, at the artefacts she had borrowed; the pieces of a life she had appropriated, unintentionally. She had believed it for a while. "Does that mean you found her?"

Hazel only smiled.

It took a long time to walk to the lough, though it was not far away. She had not walked properly in weeks, and for a moment it seemed she had forgotten how; her legs refused to coordinate, her feet were numb slabs tucked into ill-fitting shoes. Hazel wrapped a strong arm around her waist, taking her paltry weight. They looked like a couple of drunks staggering down the road, off the path and into the woods, where there was only a weak and fading moonlight to guide them. The ground was uneven; tree roots burst up through the loam, conspiring to turn their ankles, but Hazel was surefooted, guiding her towards the flat black waters of the lough. The smell of brine rose sharp in her nostrils and she welcomed it, flushing out the lingering antiseptic stink of the hospital. This, she knew, was what home smelled like.

Hazel helped her sit. Cold dew seeped through the thin cotton of her pyjamas. She was exhausted; her spine sagged, her head heavy. Her chest ached horribly with each shallow, gasping breath. "It's okay," Hazel said, lowering her down onto the grass.

47

"Lay down, if you like. Rest for a bit. They won't be long."

She felt Hazel's hands soft against her hair. The wet grass cool beneath her face. The woods stretched out before them, a thick and impenetrable copse; in the dark they looked vast and infinite.

"Look," Hazel whispered. "They're coming for you."

In the distance, between the trees, a faint golden glow. The sound of twigs snapping underfoot. Voices, indistinct but definite. A pleasant warmth leached in through her skin, slowly filling her veins like hot blood trickling through a slender needle. The light grew in intensity as they drew closer, a small sun rising in the depths of the copse. She thought she could see, as she shut her eyes against the glow, a cluster of small, slender silhouettes slipping between the trees, too-long limbs and eyes burning like stars. And a broader silhouette, a little way ahead of them, running full-pelt towards the lough; her own face, worn on strong, healthy shoulders, tear-streaked and smiling and full of life.

Who Is That On The Other Side Of You?

Timothy J Jarvis

Twenty-three days out from the camp at the foot of Mount Erebus, Croker and Learmouth were forced to kill one of the huskies. After the dogs were let off the traces at the end of the day, they would usually mill about, stay close, waiting to be fed. But that evening, one of them, Roland—piebald, grizzled, more like a wolf than a dog really, but till then docile—tore off and was gone a while. The two men kept watch for him. It was clear and bright, despite being autumn, and the sun, though low in the sky, dazzled off the snow, and Croker had to peer through his Esquimau bone goggles and Learmouth was forced to squint his one eye. It was also cold for the time of year, touching 50° below. Then, after about four hours, when the two men had pretty much given up hope, sure he must have blundered into a crevasse, the dog came yipping out of the glistering mist that mantled the ground round about.

At first he seemed fine, but then he began acting strangely, barking and howling, gyring and snapping at his own tail. He got in amongst the rest of the team and swiped at a couple of them with his claws, laying open the flank of a dog called Launcelot. Then all the huskies were off, snapping and yowling. Learmouth stood looking on, fists clenched, mouth hanging slack, panting, breath fuming in the frigid air. Croker cursed, then waded into the rabble with his rifle, clubbing the brawling dogs with the stock. Reaching Roland, he thrust the muzzle to the dog's head, fired. There was a sharp crack and a wet noise, like slop thrown from a bucket. Learmouth winced.

Crocker trudged back out of the moiling pack, nodded to Learmouth, who squinted at him.

"What should we do with the body?"

Croker frowned. "With the rations those dogs are on, if we leave it, there'll be no trace by tomorrow morning. Don't bother yourself."

II

14th January. Hugh and I have been trekking along with the Scott group for a few days. We camped by them on Ross Island, and for the present our heading is the same as theirs. I have been deliberately vague about the reasons for our expedition, given them some waffle about a geological goal to reassure them we are not competing in the race for the Pole. One night, camped in the shadow of Mount Erebus, Hugh got drunk on some of that vile gin of his and nearly sank us. He grew voluble, blathered to a gang of them about what it is we truly seek. I felt there was probably more harm in shutting him up than there was in letting him maunder on, shaking my head from time to time, sure they would assume he was delusional.

So I allowed him prattle away, about Symmes, Reynolds, and Poe, and about Agartha and Shambhala. To my surprise, one fellow, Oates, listened with seeming interest. As this Oates was a surly and morose fellow who was not much liked, there being bad blood between him and others of the expedition, particularly Scott, I did not think there was much harm in his taking Hugh seriously. But I thought I had best put him off the scent by acting up. I grabbed Hugh's gin from him, swigged at it, then began to gabble the most outrageous nonsense— tentacled creatures from the furthest voids of the cosmos who, aeons ago, flew here on membranous wings, monstrous blobs of living protoplasm that squirm in tunnels beneath the earth, and so on. Then even Oates looked disgusted, turned away.

Still, while Hugh slept off his drunk, I took the spirit from him and poured it out in the snow. When he woke, I bawled him out. He peered blearily at me and shrugged. Till he realized his gin was gone. Then he became enraged, tried to strike me, but, though we were well-matched, he was hung-over and enfeebled, and I soon put him down. Later on, when his crapulence had worn off, he snivelled and sulked.

From then on, I think the Scott party have thought us mad. For which I'm glad, really. I do not wish to share my discovery with any man. But they thought us strange anyway—twins together on an Antarctic expedition, a mission of two! Though actually, now our beards have grown out—mine is dark and Hugh's grey—the resemblance is softened a little— we could have got away with saying we were merely brothers.

I do not care they think us mad. It is they who are the mad ones—imagine risking life and limb simply to attain a geographic coordinate, a point on a map! What I seek is so much more.

One day, soon after, Oates did his best to kill a bull seal he spotted sprawled on the blue ice. It was a big brute, grey with brown mottles. Apparently one such beast the party had killed while wintering had been found, when cut open, to have a belly full of fish, mostly undigested and still edible. Hence they made a habit of hunting the seals they found, though the meat of the beasts was greasy and foul, the only parts much good for eating being the innards. Oates, perhaps trying to show his backbone, ran over to kill this seal armed only with a clasp-knife. Of course the creature took off, lolloping for its hole. Oates ran alongside, doing his best to gore it. The hide of the *thing was so tough and leathery that his blade kept glancing off. Then he stabbed down and the point went in, opening up a wound. But it was shallow— there was only pinkish thick blubber and watery ichor seeping. The seal wheeled, barked at Oates, came snuffling for him. He backed away over the frozen snow, tripped and fell on his posterior. The seal kept coming, so Oates scrambled to his feet, turned, and fled. The seal then made for its hole, slid into the water. We all jeered at Oates, even when we saw how shaken he was. Blood ran from his hand— his grip had slipped down the handle of his blade, and he had cut his fingers badly.*

Extract from the Antarctic journal of Wilson Croker

II

Hugh Learmouth and Wilson Croker met one afternoon in Dawson City, in the Yukon, in the spring of 1898, during the Klondike Gold Rush. Learmouth was from London. He'd never known his parents, was a foundling, left as a newborn in the alcove out front of Thomas Coram's hospital. He'd never know if he'd been abandoned because his parents couldn't afford to keep him, or because of the large port-wine stain birthmark, shaped like a mountain with two peaks, that marked the skin over his left eye. When he was found, there was a silver locket tucked into his swaddling, supposed a memento from his mother. Inside though, there was no portrait. Just a miniature depicting a fantastic city, spires, minarets, and gilded cupolas, gargoyles and caryatids, azure tiled roofs. Learmouth kept this on him always. He was treated well at the hospital, taught his letters and figures, and was apprenticed out to a money-lender, set up for a good trade. But, growing older, he began to know a yearning to see the world. So he lighted out one night, under the cover of darkness, went down to the West India Docks, and, after a few days pestering the seamen, found work on a cargo steamer.

He crewed boats for nearly twenty years, all over the globe. Then, in 1896, hearing reports of great riches to be had, he jumped ship in New York City and made his way, by land, to San Francisco, where he found a working berth on a steamer bound for Alaska. He got to the Yukon in the autumn of 1897. Poorly outfitted and provisioned, he had a very hard winter of it, near both starved and froze to death on the Chilkoot trail.

And he was dogged by the black name of Croker his whole time in Canada. Heard tales of a Bostonian rake, scion of a wealthy family who'd burnt through his inheritance, come out to the Yukon hoping to strike it rich and make enough to maintain his dissolute lifestyle, a man who, for all he didn't look particularly imposing, was a black-heart and a living terror to honest prospectors, the leader of a band of roughneck claim-jumpers who'd drive men off promising patches of dirt they'd staked, though not till after they had done the hard work of thawing out the ground. A man who was said finally to have quarrelled with his mates over the spoils and slaughtered them all, seven hefty brutes, carved them up with his Bowie knife, neat as jointing fowls, and buried the pieces in the cold Alaskan earth. A man who, many folk told Learmouth, was the spit of him, save for his birthmark. Many times he was cussed and threatened by those Croker had wronged. Most times his birthmark and his British accent saved him a beating, but he'd lost teeth and had ribs broken in Croker's stead. Then he'd lost his left eye, gouged out during a brawl with a thug in the tent city on the shores of Lake Bennett. The thug had mistaken Learmouth for Croker.

Learmouth ended up with little to show for his toils and hardships beyond a few small nuggets of placer gold and a reputation for being a vicious sneak, after he'd stolen into the thug's tent while the man was sleeping and opened him up from crotch to craw. The gold he sold on arriving in Dawson, and he squandered all the earnings on drink and boys and gambling, and drink before all; the reputation, though, he couldn't get rid of. Folk wouldn't loan him anything, and, as he was in a hole, he had no idea how he was going to get out of the Klondike.

In spite of everything, Learmouth believed his resemblance to Croker could only be superficial— whoever heard of a man having a true double who wasn't a twin? And though he knew nothing of his kin, he couldn't see how any brother of his could have ended up being raised by wealthy New Englanders when he'd been left at the door of a foundling hospital in London.

So he was confounded, on entering the Grizzly's Head that afternoon—gone in to find a poker game, hoping with his last dollars to win big enough to be able to get out of the city—to see, sitting beneath the moth-eaten taxidermy mount that gave the low saloon its name, a man who had his face, though less ravaged.

Learmouth crossed over. "You Croker?"

"Good Lord!" the man exclaimed. He had a simpering lisp that fitted his foppish air and manner of dressing, though not his frame, which, like Learmouth's, was, if scrawny, tough and sinewy. "Yes, that I am. And who might you be?"

"Name's Hugh Learmouth. Folk keep mistaking me for you."

"I shouldn't wonder. It's remarkable!"

54

"It is that."

"Have you ever read Poe? "William Wilson"?"

"I've not."

"Well you should. Have a drink with me?"

They sat and shared a bottle of the rotgut they served in that hole. Learmouth had thought he'd feel murderous should he ever encounter Croker, but in the event he was stunned by the likeness and forgot what he'd gone through because of it. It wasn't perfect—apart from Learmouth's birthmark and, of course, his missing eye, Croker's jawline was slightly stronger, Learmouth's brows more beetling—but it was eerily close.

Though his rage was routed by wonder, Learmouth didn't really take to Croker; but after a few shots they got on well enough, told each other tales of how they'd come to end up there.

At one point Croker asked Learmouth about his eyepatch, and Learmouth told him the story of his lost eye, with only a trace of rancour, lifted the patch to show his hollow socket. In it, Croker saw a vision of something he'd been seeking for many years—an entrance to that place known as Agartha, the fabled inner lands. He thought it very beautiful and knew then he wanted to make Learmouth his. He was inflamed by the prospect of a lover who was a near mirror.

Later they played poker, and one of the other men at the table cheated, and Croker and Learmouth caught him at it, took him out into the street and broke his skull for him. After that, they went for a drink in another saloon on the strip. An hour or so after, while Learmouth, who was drinking more heavily, was pretty loaded, was using the jakes, Croker tipped a powder of Spanish fly, dried lemur gland, and fossilized horn into his drink. Then he incanted some words over the drink, words he'd learned from a Tunguska shaman. Returning to the table, Learmouth drained his glass, called for another slug. Half an hour later, he started to gaze at Croker, smitten. Croker then took the other man back to his room. Though Croker used him ill, Learmouth submitted and begged for more—it was a powerful magic.

♊

From that point on, Croker and Learmouth were inseparable. Soon after, they set out for the gold fields again. By the time the summer was out, they and their crew had passed into Yukon legend, known for their uncanny knack of always striking paydirt wherever they dug and for their utter ruthlessness in making promising claims their own. Robert W. Service, the famous 'Bard of the Yukon', even wrote a stanza on them:

The Yukon gold fields have their bogeys,
Same as any other place,
But here they're real, will have you
On your knees,
For here evil shows its face.
The cussedest of all, names to dread,
Are Croker and Learmouth,
They've stolen many claims, broken more heads,
Driven many folk back south.
They are the spit of each other, like twins,
Save that Learmouth lacks an eye,
And has a mark, a patch of red skin,
And a great weakness for rye.
Croker they say is a sorcerer,
And in league with devils.
Dark rites are the source of his power,
And in chaos he revels.

They are worse even than "Soapy" Smith,
Have butchered families, kids and all,
For no more gold than would buy a fifth,
For kicks really, to have a ball.

Croker and Learmouth left the Yukon that autumn
rich men. Croker had come to have a certain affection
for Learmouth, beyond his lust, but he would not
release him from the spell. Learmouth, for his part,
largely hated Croker, and couldn't understand why he
was so besotted, why he felt compelled to stay with
his dark likeness.

II

The next few years they travelled the world over,
seeking riches both material and occult. They used
their incredible resemblance in a confidence trick that
supplemented the money they'd made in the
Klondike. Apart from Learmouth's port-wine stain
and missing eye, only the really observant could tell
them apart—nearly the same face, same shock of
dark hair, same build. So Croker simply used rouge
on his forehead and wore a patch. The only
noticeable difference between them then was their
gaits: Learmouth limped a little, an old injury from
when he'd been struck on the hip by the steel eye of a
rope flailing wildly in a storm; Croker shambled as if
walking were really too much effort for him.

After that they settled together in San Francisco,
in a big house on Nob Hill, posing as brothers, to rest
and enjoy their wealth and for Croker to pore over the
Hermetic tomes he'd acquired. By this time most of
Learmouth loathed Croker and the rough treatment he
meted out and would argue back, but, still bound by
the love charm, another part of him felt a bond that
couldn't be broken, even felt a fondness born of

familiarity. One thing he was grateful to Croker for, was introducing him to literature—he'd become a keen reader of fiction, especially weird tales and scientific romances. Croker, though he sought variety in the desperate street life of the vice-ridden city, perversely grew more and more in love with Learmouth, swore he'd never release him.

Then, in April 1906, the Earth shuddered and fire raged through San Francisco, and their mansion was razed. They fled the place and on returning found that all that had not burned had been taken by looters, including their safe. There was nothing left. They set out from San Francisco then, to live as hobos riding the rails. Croker grew morose. It was his near success in a ritual to open up a portal to the Hollow Earth that had caused the quake, but having lost all his occult tomes and paraphernalia he knew he'd have to start his quest over. He sulked and treated Learmouth even worse than before.

II

A few years later, Croker and Learmouth were living hand to mouth in New York, staying at a Bowery flophouse. One day Croker was looking desultorily through the stock of a second-hand bookseller on a quiet backstreet when he came across a copy of Poe's *The Narrative of Arthur Gordon Pym of Nantucket*. He'd read the book before and had found it frustrating and turgid, quite unlike the short stories, which he loved. But the title of this copy excited his curiosity. It was an 1870s British reprint, presumably a pirated edition, and the publishers had given the work an odd archaic title, *The Antick Travels of the Errant Arthur G. Pym*, picked out in gilt on the cover and spine of the green leather binding. Croker took the volume up, opened it. He found himself looking

58

at a frontispiece, a woodcut depicting an ice-bound landscape with, at its heart, the crater of a volcano that gave onto an opening in the Earth's crust. In the depths could be glimpsed the spires, minarets, and cupolas of a city of some kind. Not a scene he remembered from the novel. But, knowing that Poe had been an adherent at one time of John Cleves Symmes Jr's and Jeremiah N. Reynolds's theories of a Hollow Earth, one he'd hoped to find. The muddled ending of Poe's novel had irked him—he'd hoped for some insight, some allusion, perhaps veiled to all but the initiate, to storied Agartha, an expansion of the hints of the story, 'MS. Found in a Bottle'.

Croker began to leaf through the volume, but then felt a hand on his shoulder. He turned. The vendor, a burly fellow, stood behind, glaring. He pointed to a notice that read, 'No Browsing', then said, "Either buy it or put it back."

So with the last of some money they'd got together from doing odd jobs and from Learmouth turning tricks, Croker bought the book, took it back to the flophouse to study. He skimmed the text. Most of it was the same as that of the version he'd already read. But the last few pages were very different. Instead of an enigmatic encounter with a shrouded human figure, this version concluded with Pym meeting the legendary Prester John, being taken down into the interior of the world, and shown the wondrous sites of that place.

Once he'd finished a close perusal of these pages, Croker turned back to the etching at the book's opening. Looking again he saw the shape of the volcano was quite distinctive. It had two peaks, two craters, one dead, an entrance, the other still active. Then he realized what that twin-peaked volcano resembled.

When Learmouth came in exhausted, a bit later, he found Croker sitting on his bunk, all fired up.

"Hugh!"

A man trying to sleep in one of the other beds groaned, rolled over, and pulled his covers up over his head.

Learmouth winced. "Please. Let me sleep."

"Listen—"

"I'm too exhausted."

Croker got to his feet, and bellowed. "If you didn't drink so much perhaps you wouldn't be so knackered, you one-eyed scrag!"

The other man in the room burrowed further into his bedding—the men who shared the room with Croker and Learmouth were used to their set-tos.

"And perhaps if you weren't such a damned sluggard," Learmouth threw back, "you could do something to bring some money in!"

"I have, you damned fuddlecaps! I've found out the location of the entrance to Agartha! Untold riches will be ours!"

"What are you babbling on about?"

"Agartha! Fabled city of the Inner Earth!"

"And you've found a way in?" Learmouth shook his head and tapped his temple with his forefinger.

"I have. I have indeed."

Learmouth sighed. "Well, where is it?"

"Antarctica!"

"How do you know all this?"

"Look here." Croker opened up *The Antick Travels* to show Learmouth the woodcut. "See this? That's a depiction of the entrance. The last few pages of the book describe a journey into the Earth's innards."

Learmouth put his head in his hands. "What does that tell us? It's a work of fiction for Christ's sake!"

"I know that, idiot, but Poe knew something. The bizarre circumstance of his death tell us as much." He prodded the page. "And look again at the picture."

Learmouth peered at the illustration. "Well, the volcano has two peaks. It's shaped like... Oh."

"Exactly! It's the very image of your birthmark. With your empty eye socket like the dead crater. It's got to be a sign!"

Learmouth didn't tell Croker how closely the city in the woodcut resembled the one in his locket, but that struck him too.

"Maybe. But how in Hell are we supposed to get to Antarctica?"

"I've a wealthy uncle I'm due to inherit from. He's nearly seventy, though still hale and hearty. But we can always help him on his way."

"What? Then why have we been living in poverty these last years—"

"Hush, my sweet."

"No, I won't hush, you—"

Croker silenced Learmouth with a kiss. And the man who'd been trying to sleep groaned, got up, and left the dormitory.

♊

The spell meant Learmouth felt compelled to accompany Croker on his Antarctic expedition. But even if it hadn't, he might still have gone along. He'd caught some of Croker's enthusiasm, begun to believe in the existence of Agartha himself, and that they would find an entrance to it.

♊

Croker had been wrong. There were traces of Roland's carcass when the two men roused themselves to get going the following day. Though little more, it's true, than gnawed and scattered bones with a few shreds of flesh clinging to them, some scraps of hide, wet fur, a patch of snow mottled pink, red, and black. Learmouth was out first. He'd seen much in his life, and generally had a strong constitution, but during the night, while Croker had been sleeping, he'd sneaked a good few slugs of gin from a flask he kept stashed in the medicine kit, and felt a touch fragile. So sighting Roland's remains turned his stomach, and he had to stagger behind the tent and puke a thin bile. It trickled looping onto the snow, making a yellow sigil against the white. He hoped Croker wouldn't notice.

They breakfasted, then broke camp. It was another clear day, and overhead the sun was dogged by a hazy double. It was also strangely still, all wind had died. But it was very cold again. Handling rope—lashing up the tent and the sleeping bags, tying things down to the sledge—was bad enough, worse was dealing with the strings that bound up the provisions, which were frozen stiff, and worse still was handling metal—the Primus and oil can, the mugs and spoons, the buckles that fastened the straps over the supplies when the sledges were loaded. But they got on, then toggled up the dogs' harnesses to the traces and set off.

They could tell, by long depressions in the snow like shallow trenches, that the ground they were traversing was heavily crevassed. But the rifts were arrayed in lines, and by travelling with them, which was roughly their heading, Croker and Learmouth were able to make good progress.

But then they came to a fissure that ran at right angles to the others. Croker's team and sledge sailed over it, but Learmouth's lead dog, Guinevere, fell through the crust and into the cleft. Luckily the other dogs saw, skidded to a halt, and Learmouth was alert, swift in throwing out a braking anchor, which caught and held, bringing his sledge to a jarring stop. He yelled to Croker. Then, getting down, he crossed over to the crevasse, looked in, and saw Guinevere whimpering, dangling in her harness at the end of the trace.

Learmouth could see the dog was badly injured—a bright spur of bone jutted from her foreleg, and blood ran from the wound, spattering the ice far below with weird symbols. He began hauling her up by the leather strap. Unable to get a firm grip with his gloves on, he took them off.

Croker, who'd turned his sledge back on hearing Learmouth's cry, stopped, trudged over. When he saw what Learmouth was doing, he bawled, "Put your gloves back on, halfwit! You'll get frostbite!"

Learmouth looked up. "Guinevere's gone in. Help me Wilson."

Croker approached the crevasse from the other side, looked down. "Christ man, the bitch is good as dead anyway. Look at her leg."

The rift was narrow. Croker took his Bowie knife from his pack, stretched out, and sawed through the taut and thrumming trace. The dog fell. Learmouth looked away. Guinevere's yowl was cut off with a crunch when she struck the packed ice.

The two men went on.

II

Later that day they heard a yap from behind and turning saw a husky scampering along after. It dogged them for several hours, though never drew very near. Then it stopped, gave a long hoarse howl, and loped off the way it had come.

That evening, after they'd pitched their tent, and were sat inside waiting for some cornmeal and water to warm in the cooker on the Primus, Learmouth turned to Croker.

"That dog," he said.

Slow bubbles began rising to the surface of the gruel. Croker gave it a stir with his tin spoon.

"Yes?" he said.

"Well, what do you think it was?"

"I don't think we were hallucinating, if that's what you mean." He rubbed his beard. "Her injuries were obviously not as bad as they appeared. She must have found a way out of the crevasse, come after us."

Learmouth looked up sharply. "It wasn't Guinevere."

"Of course it was."

"No. Too big. And I recognized the markings."

"Yes?"

"It was Roland."

Croker spooned some of the gruel into Learmouth's mug, handed it to him.

"Rot. Utter rot. Now eat your slop."

♊

It was clear again the following morning as they broke camp, and the sun again had a pale twin. But not long after they'd started on their way, it grew overcast, and the temperature dropped even further. The wind got up, squalls blowing snow in from the east. Mid-morning, the strange dog trailed them again, but only for about an hour, before seemingly losing interest and running off. They encountered no crevasses, but the plain they were traversing was bleak—featureless save drifts of snow, an ice-bound grey waste to the horizon.

Then, looming out of the flurries in the distance ahead, was a mountain with two peaks.

Croker crowed, pointed to it, then sank his hook, gestured to Learmouth to do the same. After both sledges had come scudding to a halt he yelled over the keening of the gusts, "That's it! That's where we're headed! We'll soon see Agartha!"

Learmouth nodded, but he could not share Croker's delight. The harsh conditions had broken his will. His breath had frosted on the fur of his hood, and it was rough, scraped at his skin. One of his eye teeth had shattered in the cold, leaving it a throbbing stub. And his one eye was sore—he was fearful of getting frostbite in it and losing his sight altogether.

"Wilson," Learmouth shouted. "I need to stop, rest, get warm. This cold has done me in."

But Croker wasn't listening. He gazed at the distant peaks, in rapture. Then he pointed. "Will you look at that!"

Learmouth followed Croker's finger. "I see it Wilson. It's a mountain. Unusually shaped, yes, but we don't know yet if it's anything more than that."

"You don't see the city?"

"City, what city?"

"The spires and minarets and cupolas! The walls and towers! The gargoyles and caryatids! The fragrant gardens with their sinuous rills! The stately pleasure-domes!"

"Where? What are you talking about?"

Croker pointed again. "There, in the clouds above the mountain. Can't you see it?"

Learmouth shook his head. All he could see was a grey mass wracking away to the east. "Please, can we stop?"

"An hour more. Don't be so damned feeble."

So they went on.

♊

The strange mountain didn't seem to draw any closer, though they made a good pace, the dogs straining in their harnesses, the traces taut. After a short while they passed a huddle of emperor penguins. As he and Croker went by, Learmouth peered at the birds.

"Wilson," he called out after.

"What is it?"

"Those penguins. I know they're really hard to tell apart. But those birds all had exactly like scars on the left side of their breast. Scars of a distinctive sickle shape. Uncanny isn't it?"

Croker shook his head.

"Nonsense. You're imagining things."

Learmouth didn't say anything further, but he did not think it was nonsense. He had a sense something eerie and awful was soon to be upon them.

The twilight thickened, and then they saw the Aurora Australis fluttering like an oily rag against the gloom to the south. And there was another light in the sky, a brighter greenish glow sweeping back and forth, scraping at the dark clouds. Its source seemed to be on the ground quite close to them. They made for it.

When they drew near, they saw the light came from what looked a chest of some kind. They threw out their anchors, brought their sledges to a halt, and went over to examine it, leaving their dogs moiling and yapping.

The lid of the chest was propped open, and it was from inside that the bright rays shot forth. The thing was made from some strange matte grey material. When they got close enough, and Croker reached out to touch it, he found it was not burning cold, as metal would have been, that in fact it had a faint warmth. The chest was not quite square—there were a few places where hollows had been carved out of it. And it had compartments and drawers and meaningless glyphs etched all over.

Croker and Learmouth leaned over to look in. They saw there was a plate of glass laid over the opening, and that the space beneath appeared to be of very shallow depth, and empty. Then the light raked across, dazzling them, and they backed off, blinking, ghosts strobing in their vision. Learmouth kept his distance, but Croker approached again and opened one of the compartments in the side of the chest. There was meat inside, the glistening innards of some beast, and they pulsed wetly. Croker shut the door again, turned back to Learmouth.

"We'll make camp nearby. Then we can examine this again in the morning, before setting out."

II

They worked—put up the tent, untied and unrolled their reindeer bags, lit the Primus, set the cooker on top, filled again with cornmeal and water. But then, while the gruel cooked, they talked about the chest. Its weird light, reflected from the clouds, lit up the tent at intervals.

"What do you think it is, Wilson?"

"I believe it's the Ark."

"The Ark?"

Croker nodded. "Yes, the Ark of the Covenant. The chest told of in the Book of Exodus, said to hold the two stone tablets of the Ten Commandments."

"Really?"

"Yes. Of course, I don't for a second believe any of that stuff about the tablets, laws handed down from God to Moses. But I believe the Ark was a powerful magical artefact. *Is*. You saw that thing out

67

there, what it's like. It defies all rational explanation."

The sweeping light lit Croker's features, then passed, freezing him in a mask of agitation.

"It's strange, true. But why would the Ark have ended up here?"

"Some say it passed into the hands of the Templars. I would say a group were transporting it to Agartha when something happened, and it's remained out here ever since, the folk of that fabled city little suspecting it lay so close at hand."

The gruel began to gurgle and Learmouth began dishing it out.

"It all sounds rather far fetched to me."

"Really. What do you think it is then?"

Learmouth mused a moment. "I think it might be one of them Martians that H.G. Wells fellow has written about."

Croker snorted. "Right."

"Well, you've seen it."

"Indeed I have. Anyway, it's probably useless to speculate further. We'll just have to examine it more closely in the morning."

II

But in the morning, which was clear and dry again, the chest was gone. And completely inexplicable, so was the mountain with the two peaks. More mundanely, so was a large part of their supplies. Croker raged for a time while Learmouth broke camp, but finally he calmed. Learmouth turned to him.

"We only have provisions enough to get us back to McMurdo Sound if we go directly."

Croker nodded.

"My guess is," Learmouth went on, "whoever took our supplies knew this. It was a warning. I think we should heed it, make our way straight back."

Croker grimaced and balled his fists, but finally nodded.

"There's something I must do before we get off, though."

"We've not time."

Croker struck Learmouth in the mouth, split his lip. Learmouth leant over and drooled bloody slobber; drivelling on the snow, it traced an ankh.

Croker went on. "This is important. Which of the dogs will we least miss?"

"We can't spare any of them."

"We'll have to spare one. So which is it to be?"

Learmouth crossed his arms. "Wilson, we can't spare any."

Croker went to the pack and seized up a bitch called Morgan le Fay; he knew her to be one of Learmouth's favourites. "This one then?" He took out his Bowie knife and held it to the dog's throat.

"Please," Learmouth groaned. "Not her."

"All right," Croker said, then let the bitch go and grabbed hold of another dog, Galahad. Croker hacked open the dog's throat then held him while he convulsed his life out. Then lay him on his back, slashed open his belly, tore out his innards, tossed them steaming on the snow. Peering closely, muttering and making arcane gestures with his hands, Croker stood over the ravelled guts for a time. But then he cursed, kicked the offal to the other dogs and stomped off.

Ⅱ

22ⁿᵈ February. It's three days since we saw that weird chest out on the ice and the mountain with the riven peak, then both disappeared. Croker has been even more moody than usual since. We've barely spoken and he no longer huddles up to me for warmth at night. I think he's convinced what we saw was real and we were perhaps drugged and moved, along with the tent, both sledges, far enough from the peak that it could no longer be seen above the horizon. He keeps going on about these two men who are apparently following us, but I've not seen them. Anyway, he keeps the revolver on him at all times. I'm worried he thinks I'm in cahoots with these men. He leads us by the compass, through the blank expanse, in the general direction of McMurdo Sound. I hope we reach it soon, before distrust and the loneliness crack his brain even more than it already is, and he turns on me.

I'm not sure what happened to us. Perhaps we dreamed it all. Maybe those things were visions brought on by too much occult lore, too much Jules Verne, of whose work Croker is very fond. I hate it, find it dull as ditchwater, but have had enough of it inflicted on me that some of those boring ideas have wormed their way into my brain. Verne has no imagination, it's all so prosaic. Strange that Croker, who is so obsessed with the eldritch, is compelled by that tedious stuff.

I've not seen any men behind us, but I've seen Roland again, padding after us, have heard him howling.

Extract from the Antarctic journal of Hugh Learmouth

♊

22nd February. I cannot understand what happened to us, how we and all of our things were moved without us being aware of it. But there can be no other explanation. Hugh asserts we hallucinated the whole thing, but he is a fool; I am certain the Ark, the mountain were real.

I have seen those two men following behind us again. Of course the terrain, a gently undulating plain of snow, would make concealment difficult, but, even considering this, they are brazen, make no attempt at stealth, though they keep their distance, do not approach. They must have had something to do with what happened to us.

Hugh still claims not to see them. I think my spell still holds, but I'm worried—something is not right. I attempted divination using haruspicy the morning we woke to find the mountain, the Ark, our supplies gone, but it would not work. I fear my powers have deserted me. I must be wary.

Extract from the Antarctic journal of Wilson Croker

II

29th February. I'm writing this tucked into my reindeer bag, by the glow of the Primus. It's ten days since we turned back. We should have reached McMurdo Sound by now. We're lost out here. Wilson doesn't seem worried, but, though we've tried to eke out our rations, we're almost out, have three or four days' worth left at most. And the going's been slow and hard. There are crevasses to look out for, and we've griping spasms in our guts, thin bloody stools, and the cold has fucked us—we can't stop shivering, half the toes on Wilson's left foot are black and shrivelled, and the tip of my nose is the same dead hue. Jesus Christ what a mess!

Earlier, after the sun had dropped down, Wilson tore off a strip of awning, wrapped it round a tent

71

pole, soaked it in paraffin, set it alight, held it aloft. A guttering flame, black choking billows. He looked about, scanning the horizon.

"Wilson," I said. "What are you doing?"

He just scowled, but then, quickening, pointed back the way we'd come. "There!" he cried. "They answer us. Who are they?"

I followed his finger, but couldn't see anything.

(Some time later) I've been trying to get some shut-eye, and I think I dozed a bit, but then Wilson started talking in his sleep. He mumbles—I can't make much out, but he talked about those he believes follow us and said my name a few times.

He's just given a drawn-out whimper, then said, "I'm so scared. We're lost."

We shouldn't ever have come here. I could almost pity Croker, if I didn't hate him so much. But I'm sorry for myself for his loss of nerve—the old Wilson would have known how to get us out of this. I should just ring the pompous bastard's neck. But that would be like throttling myself. And, besides, in spite of everything, I guess I still love him. Enough anyway.

Extract from the Antarctic journal of Hugh Learmouth

II

30th February. I do not know why those others responded to my flare last night, though I had an inkling they might. I am certain they mean us harm, not good, but I cannot understand why they toy with us, do not descend upon us and make an end of things. Learmouth continues to maintain he does not see them. I cannot understand it. Their torch last night was plain as plain.

Extract from the Antarctic journal of Wilson Croker

♊

30th February. I'd thought Wilson mad or gulling me, but today I finally saw the men following us, the men he's been ranting on about these last days. It happened while Wilson was feeding the dogs a few meagre hunks of frozen salted beef. The poor beasts are even more gaunt and pitiful than we are. I don't think they'll last much longer.

But as Wilson threw the meat to them, and they gathered whining and weakly butting heads, I happened to look west, to where a dull reddish sun hung low and feeble in the sky. And stark against it were the dark forms of two men and a dog. They must have been standing on a ridge for as they came towards us they sank down into the landscape and couldn't be seen any more. I don't understand. There's no way they could keep pace with us, if they're on foot. The gaits of both men were pretty familiar, though I couldn't quite place them.

I keep thinking of the first man I loved, I mean truly loved. He was the Boatswain's Mate on the second ship I ever sailed on, the SS Erl King. He was kind. Perhaps the kindest person I've ever known. He sometimes had trouble getting his words out, would stutter and stammer, and at first the men mocked him for it. They soon learnt not to though, 'cause he could be fierce. He was gentle with me, though. But I was cruel in those days. When I left that ship for another, I stole from him. One of the things I took was a silver mirror that had belonged to his dead sister. Somehow, a few years later, he found out where I was living, sent a letter to me. He wrote that I'd broken his heart. I never replied.

Something very odd is going on. This is all a load of horrors isn't it? I don't know if Wilson's in on it or not. Why do I still care about the arsehole so? Basically everything is ballocksed. Part of me thinks death can't come soon enough.

Extract from the Antarctic journal of Hugh Learmouth

♊

31ˢᵗ February. With these bright clear skies, the snow-glare makes it difficult to use the telescope, but earlier, squinting through it, my goggles still on, I made out the face of one of the men tracking us. Things grow stranger. For, though Hugh stood nearby me as I scanned the plain behind with the glass, I could swear that face was his. Or mine, I suppose, but that man out there had a port-wine stain in the shape of a mountain with two peaks, an eyepatch, a grizzled beard. What is happening to us? Perhaps we are going mad in the blinding nothing of this Antarctic waste. Perhaps Hugh is right? Or is something else happening? Doubles and doppelgängers—it is like a German fairytale.

I keep thinking about my mother. She used to read me Brothers Grimm before bedtime. Christ how she stifled me with her love. When I got a bit older, I used to dread the nights when my father was away on business, or out with one of his mistresses, and she would come into my room when she thought I was sleeping and stand at the end of my bed watching me. After Father died, it got worse. I was so glad when she killed herself. Who drinks lye because the signs of age are starting to show? Vain, stupid woman. After the funeral, I burned every portrait of her in the house.

Learmouth and I have been careless, let the frostbite get a hold. Even if we make it out of this, our hands and feet will be left useless lumps of flesh, like ham hocks, and our faces will be left skulls. This is a screaming fiasco, is it not?

Extract from the Antarctic journal of Wilson Croker

♊

That night, squalls blew in from the east. After he'd been asleep a short while, Learmouth was awakened by a noise, a fluttering as of a wounded bird coming from outside the tent, just audible over the wonted sounds—the boom of gusts billowing the canvas of the tent and keening in the stays. Croker was still sleeping beside him. Learmouth wriggled out of his bag and crawled over to the door. He unfastened the flaps, struggling with the lashings, which, frozen, were like wire, and looked out into the swirling snow and biting wind. Peering in the half-light, he saw the source of the noise—a sheet of paper that had become wrapped around one of the guys. He reached out and snatched it, backed into the tent, lashed everything up, and got back into his bag. Croker snored on. Learmouth examined the paper by the light of the Primus stove they'd left burning low.

It was covered in writing in pencil in a crabbed wavery hand. Learmouth had to peer to make it out. It read:

1st March. The snow is falling so thickly that all is white, and you cannot see your hand in front of your face. These horrid circumstances mean any attempt to go on would be fatal. But there is little chance for Titus unless we can go on soon. He lies on

75

his pallet, in his reindeer bag, a sheen of sweat on his brow. There is a high cloying stink about him. He will not let anyone take a look at his feet, but we know his toes are ashen with rot. He has mettle, for all that he is a fool, keeps lucid, where most men would be begging the nepenthes of morphine. But he does from time to time grow delirious and rambling. Then he squirms in his bag and talks about a seal he tried to kill and how it had had the face of a bully, a boy who had tormented him at Eton. Or he curses 'the blasted Boers,' for the gammy leg they gave him. At times he calls for a 'little Ettie.' At others he sleeps.

He is a dead man anyway and a drain on our meagre supplies. Sometimes I think I should just stave his skull with an ice-axe and throw the body to the starving dogs.

But I would not do anything so lacking in honour. That cad Shackleton, he would do it! But not I.

I wonder what happened to those queer fellows from the McMurdo Camp. All that talk of an Inner Earth. At the time, I thought it so much rot, the kind of nonsense that ghastly man Crowley spouted at me when he cornered me at a soirée that time. But now I am not so sure. These last weeks I have seen skittering shapes out in the diamond dust on clear days, and now out in the blizzard, since it began to snow; I have seen weird shadows on the canvas of the tent, and nothing there when I look outside…

Learmouth pondered that a moment, then folded the sheet and tucked it into the front pocket of his knapsack, fell back into a doze.

He awoke, what could only have been a short time later, with a weight on him, struggling to catch his breath. Croker knelt on his chest, stared down at him with bloodshot malice, mouth hanging slack, swagged with drool. Learmouth struggled, struck out with his fists, but Croker took the blows, seemed not to feel them. Then he reached down, put his hands round Learmouth's throat, and pushed with his thumbs into Learmouth's windpipe. Learmouth's sight hazed and began to go dark. He struggled, desperate, flailed, scrabbled about on the ground beside his bedroll. Then, laying his right hand on it, he thrust the Primus into Croker's face. There was a frizzle, the stench of burning flesh and hair, and Croker hissed, flinched back. Then turned and crawled out of the tent.

Learmouth set the stove down, sat up, choking and spluttering. When he'd got his wind back, he put on his jacket, trousers, cap, gloves, and boots, reached into his pack, pulled out his Bowie knife, and got up, left the tent.

Outside, peering at him, dazed, dressed only in his woollen underwear, stood Croker. He began to speak, but Learmouth stabbed him twice in the neck. Blood welled and seethed, and Croker sank to his haunches. He was struggling to speak, a horrid gurgling in his throat, but Learmouth could make out that he mouthed, "Who is that on the other side of you?"

Turning, Learmouth saw, red-eyed and laughing, a man who was his twin stood behind him. This double grinned nastily, then backed off, was joined by another man, his face in shadow. Then they went off cackling, one limping, one shambling.

Learmouth turned back to Croker, went to stem the flow of blood, but it kept bubbling through his wool-clad fingers, till it grew sluggish and cold, and Croker died on his knees in the snow, wearing a breastplate of frozen gore.

Tears running from his eye and socket, freezing on his cheeks, Learmouth lurched off through the snow. He left the campsite far behind. His blood-sodden gloves stiffened into claws. At first the cold gnawed at his extremities, and he shivered and shuddered as he staggered along, but then a strange flush of numb warmth flooded him, like the first good tot of gin after a while. Then he saw a beam of light sweeping back and forth before him, made for it. When he came to the weird chest, he lay on its glass and pulled its lid down on top of him.

II

One of the groups of Norwegians we talked to, I cannot remember their names now, reported having seen something very odd out to the west of the Sound. They said they saw a plume of gore spurting from the tongue of a glacier there and made for it to investigate. The oddest thing they had ever seen, but soon to be eclipsed, for, as they neared the blood falls, they saw about fifty or sixty men, yet all the same man, all identical, all dressed in blood-stained woollen gear, all with one mad staring eye, the other eye a raw hole, a large red birthmark on the forehead, all with faces mottled with necrosis, come haring over the glacier and, like swarming lemmings, all go over the edge into the water. They flailed there for a bit, but quite swift sunk below the waves.

Most of the Norwegians were fairly mazed by this, and began to wonder if some of their victuals had been tainted. One of them though, nodded sagely and spoke of the fey and of changelings.

Some years later, I heard tell of a man who had been with Shackleton in 1907-'09 who had come back looking much the same, but so different in manner that none of his family or friends knew him, more greatly changed than even an Antarctic trip could explain.

I do not know what to make of all this. I only know there are more mysteries to that place than man will ever get to the bottom of in a million years of exploration. And I would not wish it any other way. The shopkeeper may gain a comfort from knowing the contents of his stockroom, but it is a paltry and banal kind of comfort—give me the wonder of an infinitely insoluble universe any day.

An extract, cut from the published book, of the manuscript of Apsley Cherry-Garrard's *The Worst Journey in the World*

What's Yours Is Mine

Holly Ice

Crouched on the stone doorstep, I lifted the silver letterbox lid to peer inside.

A car honked as it roared through the slush behind and I slipped on the morning ice, head-butting the letterbox's lip of frosty metal. It scratched but I pushed forward and squinted into the unlit hallway. The house keys had fallen from the keyhole into Mum's slipper on the cheesy *Home Sweet Home* doormat; the other slipper was a potent spot of pink on the beige carpet, adrift near the living room.

I placed my mouth over the letterbox and cupped my hands to carry my voice. "Mum? You okay?"

Nothing. I snapped the letterbox shut, my knuckles already red from knocking. I had keys— Mum and I grinning on the keyring after my first cross-country race—but I hated using them. Still, I twisted the lock and let myself in, not for the first time this month.

"Mum?"

I plucked her keys from the slipper and set them by the fake plant on the hall table along with my bag, then headed into the house, shedding my scarf and coat. "Are you in here, Mum… Grace?"

Something thumped in the living room and her old leather chair groaned. Mum soon peeked around the door, favouring her good hip. She swung her regulation NHS cane at my head.

I dodged the grey stick and put my hands out to placate her. "Mum, it's me."

The cane paused at waist height and she rubbed her bad hip through her jeans. "Who are you, and how the hell did you get in?"

"I had keys. It's me, Sophie."

"Get out." Her nose flared and she barred the stairs. Her cane prodded the air, inches from my lips, with no hint of a shake in her arm. "My little ones are upstairs, and I will fight you."

I closed my eyes. She was having another bad day. "Grace, it's okay. Your carer sent me. You know Karen, right?"

Mum's cane stilled, but she nodded, a tightness leaving her lips. "I know Karen."

"Good. Let's get a brew in us. You sit down."

Mum lowered her cane and edged toward the living room, and the landline. She kept a healthy space between us, despite her hip. "You know where to find the mugs?"

"Yes, Grace."

She settled into her chair and reached for the phone to check my story. Karen knew what to say.

I stored her slippers on the shelf by the door and stroked the fur trim. She could have tripped and bashed her head falling over these, and she was talking about little girls. How old was I to her now?

My hands shook as I entered the kitchen and opened the mug cupboard. I grabbed her favourite poppy meadow mug and my own: three grinning cats, mischievous as Cheshire himself. The porcelain rattled as I set them on the counter. She should have had so much more time.

I poured boiling water, plopped in the teabags, and assessed the week's damage. The counters were clean, bar a few tea stains and a saucer full of used teabags, but the kitchen table was a mess. Toast crumbs and unopened, overlapping letters competed for space.

One letter I'd thumbed through far too often had a large glob of Mum's blueberry jam occupying its window. I wiped off the gloopy sugar with a

81

dishcloth and slid the papers out. 'Office of the Public Guardian', a Victorian name for the authority that stripped someone of their rights. I must have read the number-punched documents three dozen times, but it was time to do more than arrange carers. Some of Mum's letters would be final notices for energy bills. She was more in her head than the house now; lost inside herself. I dropped the papers and rubbed my temples. Last month she'd tried to take twins from the primary school home with her. I smoothed my skirt and turned my eyes to the ceiling. If she wasn't in her fifties and greying, people might not have asked questions.

Twelve deep breaths later, I brought the steaming mugs into the living room. The phone was back in its cradle, and Mum smiled at me.

"Here you go," I said. "Your favourite mug."

As always, jumper-covered hands reached for the drink. "Not seen this one before." She stroked the poppy petals and blew on the steaming liquid, whistling through her teeth. "Pretty design, though."

"Yes, it is."

I took a seat across from Mum and waited for her to say something. Sometimes, if she was left to speak, she had moments of diamond clarity.

She eyed me through the steam. "You look like my Isabelle, but older."

"Isabelle?"

Mum gulped down tea. "My daughter." She huffed. "Did Karen not tell you anything?"

I cupped my mug and smoothed the indented lines which made the whiskers of its cats. "Your daughter's name is Sophie."

"No, that's my eldest daughter."

"I don't understand."

Mum sat taller, the springs beneath her squeaking. She placed her mug on the crooked side table and smiled at the pictures in the old display case. "I had two children, one year apart." She stretched to touch the nearest photo. Her pink nail tapped at the gap-toothed smile of a girl no more than three; Mum closed her eyes, as if remembering that day at the bouncy castle party.

"That's Sophie, Grace."

"Oh, they are near identical. Beautiful girls." Mum shook her head and stared into her tea. The clock ticked through a minute before she took another sip. "Perhaps I will visit her tomorrow."

"I thought she lived here?"

"No, not for many years."

II

The letterbox rattled as a familiar *thumpitty thump thump thump* at the door signalled the taxi's arrival. I checked the kitchen clock. One minute past twelve. Martin was always punctual, and hated waiting on the doorstep.

I pushed the brewing tea to the back of the counter and opened the door. A northerly wind stormed the corridor, but the snow was gone with last night's rain.

"Morning, Sophie." Martin scuffed his feet on the step, a habitual twitch beneath his left eye. His cap had been pulled low and shaded his weak chin and long nose. It also hid his widow's peak hairline. "Grace ready for book club?"

I put up a finger and peered into the living room. Mum was in her favourite chair, hands laced in her lap. Pictures had her spellbound again, as if my little faces watched her as much as she did them. She hadn't moved since ten this morning.

I sighed. "Best try again two weeks from now. She's devoted to that club, when she remembers."

Martin buried his hands in his pockets and nudged the doorstep with his shoe. "Mind if I come in?"

I peered over his shoulder. His taxi wasn't idling like usual. The light and the engine were out. "What's this about?"

He followed my eyes to his car and double-checked the doors were locked with the key. The car flashed its response. "Can I get off the doorstep?" He was still twisted around, watching the empty street.

I led the way to the kitchen, knowing he would rush to close and lock the front door.

Papers still heaped the kitchen table, so I swept them to the wall with one arm and pulled two chairs out. "There's another cup of tea on the counter. Mum won't miss it." I tapped the kettle for a second pot in case she did.

Martin brought both mugs over and perched on the edge of his chair, picking at the white seat cushion tassels. He didn't touch his drink, and his eye was twitching constantly. "Your mum hasn't made book club for four months."

I cupped my mug and fished out the teabag. "I know, I'm sorry it's lost you money. I can arrange services with someone else if—"

"This isn't about money. Your mother..." He met my eyes, and the twitch stopped. "Your mother asked me to tell you something if she missed the meetings for four months."

"What, why?"

"She trusted me." Tassels twisted and knotted between Martin's fingers and his shoe tapped the lino. "It wasn't a book club she was visiting."

I laughed, turning the mug between my palms. "Of course it was. She read a new book every fortnight and told me all about Mabel and Caroline, and their kids and grandkids."

"She read the books. But I promise you, I dropped her at the train station every fortnight and she caught a train."

My mug teetered on its edge, spilling hot tea over my thumb. I hissed and sucked on the throbbing skin. "Why would she lie?" I pushed the mug away and blew on my thumb. "Did you ever ask where she went?"

"Everyone knew." He scratched his stubble. "The scar, on your inner arm. That's what started it."

The crooked and pinched scar was a faded white line, vein-like as it looped from my elbow to my wrist. I'd had it since my memories were fuzzy and fragmented, before I knew what it meant to be scarred. "I got this falling off my bike."

"No, Isabelle did that. With scissors. She was three."

I sucked air through my teeth. The legs of my chair wobbled as I threw myself to my feet, and slammed the cold tap on. It thundered like a rainstorm but I only watched as the water stabbed at my scalded skin and splattered on the sides of the metal sink. *Isabelle*. That's what Mum had called my sister. She wasn't lying. Martin wasn't lying. But why ask him to tell me something like this? He might be Mum's friend, but I hardly knew him.

"What happened to her?" I traced the raised lines of my old scar. "Why would Isabelle do this?"

Martin patted my shoulder. "All kids do dumb things. Isabelle… she needed help. Your mum asked her sister to look after her, to keep you two separate."

I stopped the tap. It dripped into the plughole. "But I visited Valerie every summer."

"That's when your mother had her."

I leaned against the counter, gripping the edge, half to hold myself up and half in confusion as I struggled to make sense of this. Martin waited in the

85

room's centre, shifting his weight from one foot to the other. The twitch was back, too.

"Why did she ask you to tell me? Why not Valerie?"

"She knew she would stop visiting Isabelle once her condition progressed. You're Isabelle's next of kin now…"

I blinked and took a shaky step toward the kettle. The water was bubbling and howling out the spout. "When I was twenty, Valerie broke her leg in two places. That wasn't an accident, was it?"

"No, that was the worst of a bad two years. I took her to the hospital. Valerie insisted your mother put Isabelle in professional care. She's been at Arbury Court since."

I hurried to the kitchen table and rifled through small and large letters, ripping open their contents until I found what I was looking for: open return train tickets, dated for thirty minutes from now. I placed them on the table and carefully shunted other papers into neat piles. Linoleum creaked as Martin moved to hover over my shoulder.

"Should I call someone?"

I shook my head. "Karen will be here in an hour, and I need to think."

He gripped my arm but let go a moment later. "Sophie, anything you need. I'm around. You have my number."

I swallowed hard and patted his arm. "Thanks, but you have customers waiting." I nudged him toward the hallway. He resisted at first, and hesitated at the doorway, dragging his fingers down the frame.

"You're sure I can't call anyone?" He tapped the wood. "I know this is a bombshell to drop, especially with your mother's early onset…"

My eyes stung but I clamped my throat shut and refused to let the tears out as I waved Martin off. The front door closed with a jangle of the letterbox. I pulled the kitchen door to and leant against it for a good minute, watching the back garden's bushes lean and dance in the wind. A strong-willed tabby cat battled the gale, its fur ruffling every which way. And it settled beneath the bushes for its twice weekly dump. If mum could see him now she'd be out there in her bare feet, shooing the 'creature' from her property.

"Is the tea ready yet?" she called.

I shoved my hair into a ponytail, rubbed my cheeks, and readied myself for another hour of Mum staring at walls and telling stories about an unstable child I thought she'd imagined.

II

The car keys were a heavy weight in my lap as the engine wound down to silence. My purse sat on the passenger seat, the clasp open and the cover pulled back to show the required identity documents. I had everything I needed, but I didn't leave the car. I watched families and individuals follow the white stripes of the crossing to the red-framed glass doors fronting Arbury Court Hospital. Some smiled and chatted to their partners, others hunched and stuck their hands in their pockets, but none looked scared. A well-wrapped toddler was even making the crossing in their bobble hat. I could do this.

A rough wind rocked the car. I battled it to open the door, gripping the handle against the power of the northern chill, and reached in for my purse strap. I slung it over my shoulder and followed the white stripes, through the door, and into a white room with light wooden doors and a large reception desk.

I stopped short. The room was as clean and tidy as a dentist's office. It made me look for a crack, or a dirty spot. The worst I found was a sprinkling of soil outside its plant pot and a spot of mud on the bristly entrance matt. At least it didn't smell like a hospital; the sterile chemicals made me nauseous.

The lady behind the counter smiled, her neutral lipstick cracking. "Good morning. You must be Sophie."

"Yes." I placed my bag on the counter and pulled out my documents. "I spoke to Janet on the phone about my mother, Grace?"

The receptionist took the papers to the scanner and hiked her spectacles up her nose. "That's me. Grace... such a shame. She was here every second Sunday. A special lady, your mother."

I smoothed the glass counter, my fingertips leaving smudges of my prints. "Oh?" I eyed the keyboard through the glass, wondering how many times my mother had seen the same thing.

"Grace was forgiving and kind after every altercation and relapse. Always positive. She never gave up on Isabelle."

I traced my scar and pinched the skin at my elbow, but my mind only showed me the blurry image of my first bike. Mum's stories had taken over my memories of the incident, and I wasn't ready to broach the topic with Valerie. She still walked with a heavy limp.

"Mum is always kind, and protective."

The receptionist lifted the lid on the scanner and nudged the documents back into my hands. "That should be the last of the paperwork. After security, you can see your sister. She's really looking forward to it. And happy birthday, by the way."

I blinked. "You saw that on my ID?" I didn't think she'd checked that closely.

"No, but the tag on your blouse gave you away."

I twisted, caught the scratchy plastic sticking out my sleeve, and snapped it free.

"I don't understand." The purple silk top was a birthday present from Mum, but how could this woman know I hadn't bought it? Mum hadn't been here in months.

"Your mother tried to keep Isabelle included. Always got her a new outfit on your birthday. It... helped with her treatment."

I smoothed my top. "Can I go through security now?"

She pressed a buzzer, unlocking the wooden door to my right. "Straight through there. Debra is expecting you. She'll show you the locker for your purse."

"Great, thanks."

II

My head was reeling with security information and the nurses' names but that flew from my mind when Debra stopped outside a private meeting room. It looked the same as all the other rooms—a light wooden door surrounded by cream paint with a glass window—nothing like the horror stories of mental hospitals.

"Isabelle's waiting inside." Debra smiled and unlocked the door. "She's heard a lot about you. Just go slow. She was always fine with your mother, but she's had a few outbursts with other patients in the past."

I gave the rod-thin woman a tiny smile and pushed the door open. It clicked shut behind me.

"Mum warned me you might visit soon."

I reeled back, my heel hitting the door. Isabelle was nearly the spitting image of me. The only thing that didn't match was her eyes. The brown was a shade darker, but she had the same brown-blonde hair. It waved in the same places, and—worse—she was wearing the same outfit. I blinked and gestured to it, from head to toe. "How?"

Isabelle made the same gesture and chuckled, a throaty laugh full of rasp. "Mum liked to gift us the same outfit. She thought it was cute."

I nodded, but my tummy clenched. Cute for children, maybe. But adults? What was mum up to? I didn't even know this girl and she was like a twin.

"Maybe you should sit?" Isabelle nudged the leg of the chair in front. It scuffed the floor until a small gap was between the seat and the wooden table.

"Sure." I pulled out the chair, rumbling the legs across the Lino, and took my seat. I wasn't sure whether I should shake her hand or hug her, but Isabelle was smiling, and searching my eyes.

"I wasn't sure when I would see you again, sis. Of course, mum gave me pictures but... we really do look alike."

She laid her arms flat on the table, hands up towards me. The overhead light lit her skin, highlighting the pale line of a scar. It matched mine, in every turn and twist.

I bit my lip. "What happened there?"

"This?" Isabelle smoothed the old cut and shrugged, biting her lip in a mimic of me. She stopped when I did. "You had one, so I had one. Easy."

She grinned, and I pushed back my chair, knowing no one even halfway sane called carving their flesh easy, but she rounded the table in seconds and slammed my head down, into the table, again and again, until I saw stars and swam into darkness.

Ⅱ

90

A loud creak woke me. I sat and threw back the covers. Two nurses were chatting as they walked past, something about the latest road works. They barely glanced in my direction. The antiseptic coating my throat and swirling my stomach let me know I was in a kind of hospital but, looking around, I saw two beds and some cabinets. It was more like a dental clinic than a hospital…

My heart sped and my memories rushed in. My crazy sister had knocked me unconscious. So why was I here? Why was no one filling in paperwork, accident reports, anything?

"Excuse me, why am I here?" The nurses kept walking. "Excuse me!"

The lead nurse, the taller one, stopped and *tssked* as if I were a child. "Really, Isabelle. You would have left medium security in a month, and now your poor sister has a bump as big as yours."

The other nurse snorted. "She probably likes that."

I blinked. "She took my place." I shook my head. "You have the wrong girl. I need to leave, now."

The lead nurse rolled her eyes. "We've talked about this. It's not healthy to copy everything your sister does. Be your own person."

I swung my feet to the floor, scanning for the exits, but they'd covered each door. "Isabelle knocked me out. You can't keep me here."

The shorter nurse rolled her eyes. "She's well enough for her room. I'll take her back. And Isabelle, you know you can't leave until you're well, not after what happened with your Aunt and the other patients, and now your sister, too."

She took my arm and half pulled me through locked doors and cream coloured corridors until we reached room fifteen, Isabelle's room. The door closed behind her and I was left staring at a normal bed, already made with yellow sheets, and a wall covered with pictures, blue-tacked to the wallpaper. In each one Mum and I were at my birthday meal or coming out of a birthday movie. Every birthday from when I was a child. She'd titled the collection 'My Outings'. I rubbed my arms and sunk to sit on the bed.

"Who is this girl?" I rubbed my eyes and laid back against the wall, hoping a doctor would come soon, or another nurse, so I could explain the situation. My heart beat fast, countering my logic with panic, but I took deep breaths and waited, and waited.

I waited until dinner. Then a new nurse came to take me to the canteen. As we left Isabelle's room, she looked at me sideways. "Beverley said you were talking like your sister again."

"I came in this morning, gave you my paperwork, and you've let my sister leave instead."

The nurse paused and eyed an older nurse down the corridor. "Debra, did you check in Sophie this morning?"

Debra hurried down the hall. "Of course. Why? Is something wrong?"

The first nurse nudged my shoulder. "Isabelle sounds more level-headed than usual."

Debra eyed me and I stared back. "I don't belong here. I need to leave."

She frowned and looked over her shoulder, toward the two sets of doors which led to reception. "The sisters did look incredibly similar."

"I can prove it. This morning I talked with the receptionist—Janet—about my mother, about how kind and protective she can be, and the woman told me that my mother always bought my sister an outfit on my birthday. I even had a tag on my shirt. I had to pull it." I pulled my shirt sleeve for emphasis. A loose thread trailed down my arm.

Debra sighed. "Isabelle has been this convincing before, but I'll check with Janet. Maybe something was strange when Sophie left."

The older woman strode back down the hallway and disappeared through the doors to the outside world. I spied her through the glass, huddled over the desk as she consulted with Janet. Though I couldn't see the receptionist's face, it was obvious they were trying to keep this from the other visitors. They both paused and smiled each time Janet checked someone new into the building, as if pausing on dinner break.

Ten minutes later, Debra was done and half-jogged down the hall, red in the face. "One last question. What's your home phone number?"

I blinked. Isabelle would never have had that. I recited all eleven digits.

Eyes wide, Debra shook her head at my escorting nurse. "We made a mistake." She faced me. "I don't have words. I'm so, so sorry Sophie. I'll take you through to reception."

The other nurse stiffened but let me leave with Debra. She took me to Janet, who was staring at the automatic doors. "You two look so similar, you know. I didn't think anything of her struggling to start the car or find the keys in your purse. I thought you were out of sorts after meeting your sister, emotional, maybe angry. I never thought something like this."

Debra huffed, but she was also staring into the dark car park. "I should have made the staff more aware. Isabelle has always tried to convince us that she's you. This gave her the perfect opportunity to do just that. She must have ditched her medication somehow."

I saw my empty car parking space, and it hit me. That imposter took my purse, my important documents, my car, and left me in a mental hospital. All after cutting my arm open as a child. My teeth clenched and I took a long, deep breath. "I need a taxi." I gave them the number, knowing Martin would make me his top priority. I needed to see the state of my house. Isabelle was in the perfect position to steal my life.

Over an hour later, Martin pulled up in the parking lot. I'd been kept busy with hot chocolate, complimentary food, and insistent police questions I couldn't answer, but the fussing nurses were an incompetent, gossiping pain. I didn't want to know how much trouble my sister had been over the years or hear them tell the police she could be a danger to others. I wanted my car, my documents, and my house keys. And I wanted to go home. I also wanted more paracetamol. My head was throbbing like I'd not drunk anything all day.

I squeezed my eyes shut and stood, swaying a little as colours overtook my vision. "That's my taxi."

Janet nodded. "Leave your sister to us. The police have been informed and have her information and yours. I'm sure she'll be found soon."

I snorted. "Just don't detain me again." I set my mug down on the reception desk and swept through the doors, pulling my jacket around me against the harsh wind.

Martin wound down his window and whistled. "That's a corker of a bruise you've got."

I opened the passenger door and slammed it shut, snapping my seatbelt on with a frown. "Tell me about it. But that's not what I'm worried about. Drive me home?"

Ⅱ

"Want me to come in with you?"

The streetlamp lit the path to the door but the lights in the kitchen were on, and I'd left when it was still light. Someone had been home, and it wasn't me. "Could you wait in the car for ten minutes?" I counted out his pay, and some extra.

"Sure, I can do that. You're sure you're okay going in alone?"

I nodded and headed for the front door. I didn't have keys anymore, but I tried the lock anyway. It opened on my first try. Unlocked. I pushed it open and let the door hit the wall before I stepped inside.

All the lights were on in the hall, too, and the small downstairs bathroom. Nothing was out of place. But when I found the living room, all the pictures of me and Mum were gone, their empty frames left on the sides.

I rubbed my chest, my eyes tearing up, and my insides wringing like damp dish towels. I turned in a circle. Absolutely heartless. That's what she was. Every single picture was gone, even the ones with me and my friends. I climbed the stairs, breathing faster, and checked my bedroom. The covers had been pulled back and rumpled, as if someone had slept there, and all the pictures in here were empty frames, too.

The en suite bathroom was the last room to check. I peeked around the door but saw no shadows, and no one was inside. That wasn't the problem, the problem was it was empty. My shampoo, scissors, tweezers, makeup—hell, even my toothbrush and toothpaste were missing! This Isabelle should be in maximum security. How had they downgraded this psychopath?

I rubbed my eyes and gasped in breaths until I heard Martin turn from the driveway and rumble

95

down the main road. I was alone, in my house, and yet it wasn't my house anymore. Isabelle had taken all the personality out and left me with a shell. She could have seen or taken anything.

Squeaks accompanied the bedside drawer as I yanked it open. I rummaged through the reading material and stationery. All my latest books were still there, but my diary was gone.

I thundered down the stairs for the landline since even my mobile was gone, and I dialled 999. The police put me through to the person working Isabelle's case, but they got as far as "Good evening" before I broke down and collapsed into the living room chair, bawling.

Something crunched beneath me as I leaned back. It was a note, scrawled in a messy hand 'Sorry sis, I had to. Sharing is caring—Sophie Xx.'

The Insider

Neil Williamson

"For fuck's sake, Raymond."

He looked up from his phone, surprised at Verity's tone, even considering how badly the meeting had gone. And *badly* was an understatement. They'd flown out to Italy expecting, minimum, to negotiate a maintenance extension but planning to nudge the customer to another block of user licences and maybe a couple of feature add-ons. Three hours in that blast chiller of a conference room and somehow they'd lost one of their longest standing European clients. Obviously, it was a poach, and they'd have known if any of the usual competitors had been sniffing around, so it had to be some new mob: in the field five minutes, unencumbered by anything as inconvenient as a reputation and offering all the bells and whistles at half the going rate. In today's market even previously loyal customers would be tempted. It was obvious now that the only reason he and Verity had been flown all the way to Pisa was to be shown the door and administered a colossal kick in the arse on the way out. You just never knew with some people.

Now they were in the hotel bar, sweating in the summer swelter but still aircon-frozen inside like a pair of meat Alaskas, and using grappa and the blessed isolation of their social networks as an excuse not to be the one to write that email, not yet. It'd been a bad day but that was no excuse.

"That's a bit strong, pal. They'd made up their minds before we got here. You ken that, eh?"

Verity's look could have melted a glacier. He felt the old churn in his belly. Seventeen years in

Bedfordshire had flattened his big, round vowels like burst fitbas and all but scrubbed the Doric out of his vocabulary, but he had never fully assimilated. Being tall and awkward made him an obstacle, often in people's way. Difficult to understand too, when it suited them. Never anything wrong with his work, of course, but somehow when it came to promotion someone else was always just a little more suited to the role. Verity had been his boss for just over a year. Before her it had been Afsal. Back at the start, Harriet. He'd accompanied them all on trips like these. The dependable aide-de-camp. And, of course, whenever it all went south, as it invariably did in sales, he'd got to be the fall guy for all of them too. The scapegoat.

Verity had done all right by him so far, but what did he know about her beyond prospects and pipelines and her public page on Facebook? Even after a year of working together. He'd just been beginning to relax too.

"I don't mean the fucking I-ties." Verity swiped to the top of her screen. "I mean this fucking shit."

She thrust her phone under his nose. Showed him a Twitter thread, a pile on. Some friend had made a comment about a movie. Just a summer blockbuster that Raymond had seen and enjoyed well enough, but this friend has had a moan about the female character, her costume, the sexualised eye-candy nature of her role in the story. Typical social media griping. No, *griping* was unfair. Raymond got it, he supposed. He understood what they were saying, but… those kinds of movies were just fluff, weren't they? Some people took everything too seriously. Several of the lassie's friends had chimed in, agreeing and amplifying her thoughts. And then, of course, the trolls had showed up.

Raymond stopped scrolling. "What am I…?"

Verity's scald hadn't cooled an iota. "Keep going."

Raymond flicked down, and down. And then he saw it: his avatar—that photo he'd taken of the Northern Lights at Scrabster—and his handle. He saw the words beside them. Words he'd seen so often on his feeds that they'd ceased to have any impact. *Feminazi. Bitch. Snowflake. Cunt.* The personal threats about coming to her town, her house. About making her pay. "What...?" He looked up at Verity again and got burned by loathing. "What is this?"

"You tell me, Raymond."

He shook his head, scrolled back through the conversation. "Verity, this isn't me," he said.

"Oh, please!" She snatched her phone back off him. Held it like it was contaminated. "At least have the balls."

"It's really not." He tapped up the app on his own phone. Showed her his stream from that morning. The most recent messages were ats on friends' threads made just now while the grappa had begun its unwinding work. The last message before that was his jokey *Pisa, I am in you* from when they'd landed. There was nothing in between. "I had my phone off and in my pocket all morning," he said. "I was sitting right beside you." Seeing the confusion warring with the outrage, he flipped to his profile page and asked her to do the same for the account that looked so much like his. There were differences, and they were not even tiny ones, as if whoever had spoofed his account couldn't be arsed carrying the job through properly. The clincher, though, was the user name: *@donsloon83*. The one on her phone had an underscore on the end. You'd hardly notice it was there, but it made all the difference.

"What the fuck?" She stared at the phones so she didn't have to look him in the eye. "You could have two accounts..." But she wasn't sure now.

"Verity, I was sitting right there with you. All morning. You *ken* I never sent those messages. Someone, for some reason, has copied my account to make me look bad. Obviously it's working."

Now she looked at him. He could see that she was still a distance short of an apology, but she was coming round. "Jesus. Who would dislike you that much?"

Raymond was well enough aware that he was sometimes disliked. People just didn't seem to connect with him a lot of the time. It rarely manifested in confrontation, more a constant accumulation of little things. Like his career stagnation, and the number of times he'd heard, *you're a nice guy, but...* Dings in the paintwork, slowly, invisibly rusting through. The eddies of uncertainty swished and swirled again. He quieted it with another glug of grappa.

Verity shook her head and flicked the conversation off her screen. Done with. "You should see about getting yourself one of those blue ticks, mate."

♊

A door slam snaps him out of a doze. His eyes are gummy and his neck is stiff. His phone, still in his hand, wakes when he moves, the screen shimmering the pillows with the Twitter thread he had been reading. His imposter has been putting serious effort into dishing their shit out. To immigrants, foreigners, liberals, women, gays, transsexuals; the softer the target the better. Tossing barbs into conversations and relishing the ensuing hurt, relishing even more the bite-back from allies, going toe to toe and spluttering venom indiscriminately. Whoever they are, they've doing a fucking top job of blackening Raymond's name.

Who could dislike him that much, Verity had asked. He's been wracking his brains and can't think of a single person, but you never know what people are capable of, do you?

It's really fucking late. Raymond is no stranger to the small hours, to prowling around the house in the dark and silence. Back in the day it had irked Kez something rotten. *Why can't you just settle?* It'd been half concern, in the beginning at least. He understands that his inability to answer questions like that is one of the things that led to the separation, to the tepid limbo that would one day theoretically curdle into divorce. This though, is way beyond even Kez's ability to hold a grudge.

Even this late, it's so hot. He peels off the bed sheets. Christ almighty, they're wringing. As a rule, he hates air conditioning. Artificial coldness conjured in a hot environment, the way it makes his body feel like it's experiencing two opposite things at the same time. It has to be better than this though. He reaches for his water but finds the bottle empty, so there's really nothing for it. He pulls back the sheets and swings his legs out, clicking on the light at the same time... then freezes.

In the filament flicker he thought he saw something at the other end of the room. A scuttle, a flutter, something. But as the light steadies, his conviction crumbles. There is nothing to be seen but the contoured wallpaper. Must have been an insect, he tells himself. Got in through the window.

Naked, Raymond pads across the hotel room and opens the tiny fridge to get an Evian. He twists and drinks, trying not to gulp. The water is barely chilled.

101

Reluctantly, he turns on the aircon and stands under the rattling grille, feeling the sweat cooling on his skin even as his bones continue to steam inside him.

He can smell cigarette smoke from the street, hear laughter. Actually, no, the laughter isn't from outside. It's got that muffled quality that suggests it's from the adjacent room. Verity's.

He sighs and pads back to bed, flicking off the light again and, in the darkness, taking another drink. Still too hot for sleep, he reaches for his phone to continue reading the bile being spewed in his name. When the screen lights up again, he starts, uttering a strangled yell. On the wall, there is a pair of unblinking eyes.

Ⅱ

After dragging his luggage up to his cramped and oddly shaped hotel room, Raymond had zoned out. Too much grappa, too fast. He ought to have known better. He was just suddenly aware that the light had deepened to the warm caramel of approaching dusk, a lace-pattern shadow spread across the end wall like an umbral net. Outside there was a distant pealing of bells and the aroma of grilling meat. Raymond's stomach flipped. He wasn't sure if it was with hunger or nausea. He went to check the time on his phone but the red light was flashing. He was searching groggily for his charger when someone knocked at his door. A flurry of sharp raps.

Verity had done her hair, put make-up on—red lips, mascara, blusher underscoring the cheekbones. Applied with such determination that her face was transformed almost into a cartoon of itself. She wore drop earrings, a cocktail dress and strappy shoes, and she was not happy. "Fucking hell. I've been waiting downstairs for twenty minutes."

102

"Phone's dead." He meant in case she'd been trying to text him, not as an excuse for him messing up their dinner arrangement. "Sorry, I'm not ready."

She looked him up and down. At his sweat-marked shirt and boxers. "No kidding."

"Sorry," he said again. "Look, you go on ahead. I'll catch you up."

"No chance." Smirking, she came into his room, closing the door behind her. "You shower." She pointed in the direction of the bathroom. "I'll wait. But don't take too long."

Raymond showered quickly, his sense of himself returning as if the muzziness was a caul of jelly sluiced away in chunks by the running water. When he pulled the curtain back he found a pile of clothes neatly folded on the toilet seat. His suit and a clean business shirt instead of the jeans and red Fred Perry he'd brought as casual wear. He loved that those shirts were back in fashion though they were hellish expensive now. He thought about marching out there in his towel to claim it. Maybe that was what she wanted. A challenge.

Raymond swiped an arc of condensation from the mirror and regarded himself. The shaved head, to avoid a widow's peak. The stubble that compensated for striking out in the hair-loss lottery, the beard trimmed neat at the neckline to settle the half-hearted debate of his chin. Not that he was fat like some men got in middle age. Even for a big man, weight wasn't his problem. What he had become was soft. His pink face was doughy. His eyes, a dishwater blue. He wasn't good looking. Good looking men's social media avatars were not abstract things like photographs they'd taken. Good looking men didn't wind themselves into a frustrated, drunken funk trying to get one selfie that looked remotely acceptable for some dating app.

What Raymond could do was make himself presentable. He dried himself and put on the suit.

Verity was sitting in the chair by the window. She had been charging his phone and now she looked up, quite brazenly, from flicking through it. "Well that's an improvement at any rate," she said, unplugging the device and handing it to him. "You've got a little bit of juice now. Won't last all night, but it should do for emergencies." He knew she was talking about his phone but the way she held his gaze when she said it... *Fuck it.*

"Shall we go?" he said.

♊

Raymond blinks, and the eyes blink. He squeezes his tight shut, but when he opens them again the other eyes are still there. He wants to say they are flat on the wall like a film projection, but there is nowhere such a projection could be made from. Not the window, the angle is wrong. And anyway they aren't flat. These eyes, blue like his own but with an electric spark to them, have presence. Like someone is standing in the shadows beside the bed. Obviously, this can't be so, but Raymond finds himself unable to switch the light on to prove it. Even finding his phone where he dropped it amid the sheets and using the screen light is beyond him. He peers into the patterns of darkness, the patches and shapes, and tries to convince himself he's imagining it.

That's when he sees the lips. They're a good eighteen inches further along the wall from the eyes and as he spots them they part, revealing a strip of white like someone peeling a banana. Raymond scrambles out of bed until his back is hard against the wall.

104

"Fit like, ye feartie?" The heavily accented voice that comes from the mouth is greasy with swagger. It reminds Raymond instantly of the lads he hung about with in the city centre when he was a teenager. Their cockiness, a red-shirted blaze in Aberdeen's granite grey nineteen eighties streets. Balls too big for that dull old town. "Teasing the quines and scaring the shite oota the auld yins, eh," the voice says, as if it has been listening directly to Raymond's thoughts.

"What the actual hell?" Raymond's own voice is a squeak. He slides along the wall until the wardrobe prevents him going any further. He barely notices the MDF pressing uncomfortably against his thigh because, as he moved, more patches of shadow took form—a shoulder, a belly bulge, a hand flexing its fingers—and the relative displacement of the body parts changed too. He is reminded of a sculpture he saw once during a time-wasting afternoon in Bruges. Viewed from one angle, it was a collection of individual pieces but when you moved around it they flowed together into an apparent whole. This is like that. He is staring at a fully-embodied naked man now. At *himself.* Only, him if he were to stand taller, chest out, legs braced apart, cock and balls just swinging out there like a challenge: *come ahead ye prick.*

"How the fuck did ye end up like this, son?" The other Raymond pulls a face somewhere between disappointment and disgust.

"What do you mean?" he mumbles, because he can't make sense of the question or the questioner.

"*What do you mean*?" The mimicry is scornful. "Neebur, you're forty two years old. Ye work in a shite job and live in a shite wee hoose in a country that despises ye. Ye've nae freens, nae bird…" The words of the sudden tirade echo off the walls like a volley of slaps. "Can ye even mind when ye last got

105

your hole? Fuck's sake, man. Yer boss was layin' out the fuckin' welcome mat for ye."

"*All right.*" Is he actually having this conversation? Does he have a choice? "Going to keep your voice down? It's not that simple, is it?"

"It never fuckin' is, eh?" The other Raymond folds his arms. They look solid, muscular. There are goose pimples visible on them. "But, aye, actually it *is* that simple. Your problem, neebur, is ye care whit people think of ye. When did that start, eh? We were gallus once, us and Davo and Swanny, likes. Up the Beach End on a Saturday, running wi' the casuals, geein' the fuckin' Arabs a skelp and chasin' them a' the way hame."

"We were never casuals," Raymond's brain has belatedly engaged, asking questions, spinning through the obvious permutations regarding this impossible exchange. Dream, no. Drink, not nearly enough. Delirium brought on by the heat and potentially undercooked pork is the closest he can get to a *maybe*, but deep down, impossible or not, he knows that this is *real*. The question is whether it is *real* real or *in-his-head* real. Neither is something he wants to contemplate, but turning his back on the situation doesn't seem to be an option. "We were too young for all that," he says. "We weren't proper casuals. We were just stupid wee lads wanting to sound hard."

"So what?" The other sneers as if he's caught Raymond trying to be clever. "We were still there. We did our share. And we didn't care what any cunt thought." And he's right. As boys they had been so wild, so full of themselves. There had been nothing else for them to be. A purity in their self-absorption that had made them feel like they were untouchable. "So, I ask ye again: what the fuck happened?"

"What happened? I grew the fuck up."

106

II

They'd found a restaurant a few streets away. Family-run and not too busy. They were overdressed for the paper tablecloths and napkins but the food was good. The savoury tang of the prosciutto around the *saltimbocca* lifted both of their spirits, the velvety pleasure of the *Barolo* an order of magnitude more. When the desserts arrived, they discussed the likely repercussions of the day's disaster. It was no secret that they'd been losing more leads than they'd won for a while now. Sales slumps were a fact of life in their industry and Raymond had stopped paying much attention but, according to Verity, the directors had been getting increasingly twitchy. It was coming up for scapegoat season again.

"You're worried about where the buck stops?" he said.

"Let's just say I'm considering my options." Verity smiled archly. "And I'm not the only one this time. Rats? Ship?"

"Right." Raymond had heard this kind of talk many times before. He prodded with his spoon until the coffee in the *affogato* melted the ice cream into a lukewarm gloop then slurped a spoonful.

When the proprietor offered to open a fresh bottle of wine, Raymond put a warding hand up, but Verity overruled him. "*Per favore.*" She smiled as the man sliced the foil, then she turned to Raymond. "We fucking deserve this, and if the words *subsistence policy* are anywhere near your lips, just you suck them back down with your soup." She knocked back a good third of her replenished glass. "Don't worry, Raymond. You'll be all right." She pointed a finger at him, the lacquered nail like a glowing fire-tip. "You're always all right, aren't you?"

107

His spoon rattled in his empty glass. "What else am I supposed to do? It's called being professional."

For the second time that day, he met fierce challenge in her eyes. "You've certainly sussed out how to play the game, I'll give you that."

Raymond was wrong-footed by these sudden swings. Unsure. He tapped his phone for the time. Jesus, it felt a lot later than it was. "Look," he sighed. "I don't know what you're driving at…"

"Oh, come on. I'm your line manager. I've seen your performance appraisals, remember? You've fucked up before…"

He shook his head. Breathed out to keep his voice level. "I've been given the blame before."

"You're telling me that doesn't amount to the same thing?"

He shrugged. He knew now where all of this was leading. "Are you setting me up?"

"I wouldn't dare!" Verity arched her brows. "See, that's the funny thing. You're the one who always ends up keeping their job."

Her bluntness genuinely surprised him. "What are you actually accusing me of?"

"Me?" Verity snorted. "Nothing. But you must know that there are rumours. About Afsal, about Harriet? Some of our dear colleagues reckon you're the master of quiet word, mate."

Raymond had stopped wondering about what *other people* thought so long ago that he'd almost forgotten that his colleagues had thoughts of their own at all. One of the benefits of being in sales after all was being on the road most of the time, and away from them. "Harriet had a drink problem," he said. "It was no secret. Afsal…" Normally he would be circumspect, but fuck it, if she absolutely needed to have her bitchy curiosity sated and was really thinking of leaving anyway what did it matter? "I did

108

have a word with HR about him, off the record. He came on to me quite aggressively, several times."

"Seriously?" Verity half-laughed. She had suspected him of professional jealousy or dog-eat-dog dirty tricks, but not this. "You should have taken him up on it. Might have accidentally had some fun." Raymond sensed her mood switch again, now that she reckoned that he wasn't as much of a threat as she'd feared.

"Well, I was married at the time." He said it quietly. "And anyway, I told you, I'm a professional. At least I try to be. Getting it on with your colleagues? Just no."

Verity's gaze had distilled into something complex. "Well," she said. "That's really quite a shame."

II

"So, whit d'ye reckon?" Other Raymond places his ear against the wall behind the bed. "Did yer wee Verity get lucky in the bar down there? Is she chowing down on some salami right now? Are we going to be treated to…" he pushes vigorously on the bed to make the springs squeal, "…a' nicht?"

"Fuck's sake, shut up." Raymond knows that if this is all in his imagination all anyone will hear is him talking to himself, but he can't help responding.

"Whit?" The other's grin is mocking. "Dinnae tell me ye've no bin thinking about it?" The other him sits on the bed, stretching his legs out, one knee raised so that it's impossible for Raymond to miss that he has a semi. His skin is smooth and veined like white marble. "Ye got any pornos on here?" He has Raymond's phone and is tapping at the screen.

"What? No. Give me that." Raymond reaches out without expectation. There is no way he is going

109

to actually go over there and take the phone back. Not if it means touching him, confirming that he is really real.

"Whit? Seriously, man? No flange?"

"It's my work phone. I'd get the sack."

"Fuck's sake, neebur. Awake a' night in dego country and no even so much as a jazz mag for company? Whit are ye, a buftie now?"

"No, of course not."

"Then how did ye no just leather that boy, Afsal, the first time. Lettin' him aff wis practically an invitation to come back for another go."

"I said, shut up." Thing is, he'd expected to be repulsed by Afsal's approach. And it hadn't been aggressive like he'd told work. It had been subtle and funny and open-ended, and he'd not known what to do with it, and that was what had terrified him. "Fuck, you think my problem is sex? It's not about sex."

"What is then? What else have ye got to be concerned by? What defines ye now ye've *grown up*?"

Raymond has no answer to any of these questions.

"That's whit I thocht." The other picks up the phone again and resumes tapping and scrolling. "So, *this* is whit ye dae instead of getting' laid? Abuse cunts ye've nivver met? I'm no sayin' they mebbes dinnae deserve it, mind…"

"No." Raymond stares at his double. "That's not me. I'd rather come to the conclusion that it was you." He hadn't known he was going to say that before the words were tumbling out of his mouth but he realises it's the only way to make sense of this. If this obnoxious turd of a man is really real, then he's the only person on Earth Raymond can think of that would care enough about him to hate him.

"Is that right?" Very deliberately, the other him puts the phone down and gets off the bed. He pads over and leans his face into Raymond's so close that he can almost feel the furious breath seething from between his teeth. "Have you really thought that one through, pal?"

Raymond doesn't move, tries not to even breathe.

"Listen, son." The words are soft but heavy. Each one a depth charge sinking through the thin ice that functions as Raymond's equilibrium. Primed to go off at the slightest pressure. "Ye've lost yer way and ye need to do something about that. So, sex? Why not? Get on roond there and chap that lassie's door."

Shaking now, Raymond can't answer. The ice creaks and cracks.

"Well, you won't mind if I do then, will you?" Millimeters from contact, the other Raymond slips by him, air stroking air. Raymond watches him saunter to the dark end of the room, vanish into the patchwork of shadow. He thinks, or perhaps imagines, that the pieces drift apart again, but he can't be sure.

♊

The booze hit Verity when they left the restaurant. She stumbled and braced herself against the painted plaster wall. Under the streetlights it had the tone of sun-warmed skin. Raymond gave her a moment before asking if she was all right. She mumbled something in response that he had to ask her to repeat.

"I'm sorry," she said.

"Why are you sorry?"

"For accusing you. You're an okay bloke. I shouldn't have said those things."

They started walking back. In the empty streets, the echoes of their footsteps were like a following crowd. "The Twitter thing was pretty harsh," he said.

She pulled a wry smile. "At least you didn't say *not all men*. I mean, obviously, yes, all fucking men, all the time, you know that, right? Deep down, it's in their fucking upbringing or the Y chromosome or something. Can't help but want them though, can I?"

Raymond said nothing.

"And sorry for… you know. I thought you must have known about what people were saying but you looked so..." What? How had he looked? They were at the hotel already. "And I know it can't have been easy for you since the separation." She was just making stuff up now. He'd never talked to anyone about the separation. It wasn't easy, it wasn't difficult. It just was. He'd pushed it all down beneath the ice where it could be ignored, with everything else. Verity had stopped. He stared at her uncomprehendingly.

"I said." Her fragile smile. The wine-dark implore in her eyes. "Do you want to have another drink in the hotel bar?"

Did he? He didn't fucking *know*. She'd flirted with him and she'd accused him. What kind of choice was that to be given? "I should really get to bed."

"Please." She placed her hand, a small palm and five ember-ended fingers against his shirt. He expected it to burn like a coal but it was barely warm. Raymond flinched away from the touch anyway and her smile fractured. "Please," she said again.

Verity ordered double scotches on the company card. She raised her glass in a toast. "Fuck them all, eh?"

Raymond nodded. "Fuck everyone." The whisky would have been pretty good if the bartender hadn't ruined it by loading the glass with ice. The cubes crackled. Then he said: "It was you, wasn't it. That sold us out."

She took a sip, held it in her mouth like a hostage so she wouldn't have to respond, but then relented, swallowed and spoke a company name that Raymond had heard once or twice around the office. "That's who I'm moving to. They offered me a Range Rover. It's got touch screen."

"Fucking hell, Verity."

"I know." Then, quieter. "*I know*. It's all fucking shit. I can't tell if it was the right thing to do. I don't know anything anymore. I don't *feel* anything, you know? Sometimes I just have to do things, hit out, make something happen. Just…to *feel something*." She reached for him again. "You know what I mean, Raymond?"

Raymond downed his scotch. A confusion of fire and ice in his throat. Two things at once. Many. "Fucking hell," he said again.

II

Raymond is on the bed, listening to the wall. He doesn't hear voices or the squeak of springs. Other than the sound of his own pulse, there is nothing. Except, once, a muffled moan that may have been a sob.

What was he expecting? Already, even the notion that he has a double has melted into absurdity, but the words remain. He tries to picture himself in there with Verity. Not fucking her. He can't imagine touching her skin. Talking, then? Sharing, consoling, connecting. Not that either. He hasn't the first clue how to describe how this feels. He gets up to switch off the aircon. He's almost cold now, feels like he wants to shiver but he's not quite there. Like an itch that won't ever come into focus.

Back in bed, he returns to the incessant flow of the Western world's banality and outrage. None of it affects him. He's got fourteen fucking followers, and that's fewer than his imposter has now. How does he feel knowing that people might confuse them, think that he's the kind of person who would really say all of these abhorrent things? Honestly? He can't imagine how he would care.

Someone does, though. Verity has been taking the imposter to task. Defending Raymond's name. *A good man. A bloody good man.* Her invective is incendiary, and it hits its mark every time.

Now he can imagine her. Sitting up in bed, heart kindled by a rage that will cool too quickly when she shuts her phone down to be more than fleetingly satisfying. But while it lasts it's better than nothing.

Raymond logs out of his account, adds the underscore and logs back in with the same password. It's always been the same password and he's always known.

Hurt, the uncomplicated purity of it. It's the only feeling he understands any more.

Other People's Dreams

Stephen Bacon

Professor Braten recommended that I place a box on my kitchen table and fill it with items that keep me tethered to reality—newspapers and photographs, a journal of my day's events, scribbled post-it notes of random thoughts that might surface, even smells that evoke memory. So far no memories have returned, despite Professor Braten saying that, of all the senses, smell is the one most closely linked to memory.

I have an overwhelming fear that I will wake one morning and my progress will be lost, that I will be just like I was in the hospital in Munich all those months ago. That's the main reason for writing this—to start to build a structure of thought and personality.

Sometimes it's hard not to believe that I was born on the 2nd December 2015—the day I awoke in hospital, exactly a week after the Nuremberg terrorist attack. One hundred and eleven people lost their lives that day but it feels like that's the day mine began.

II

Professor Braten speaks in that clipped German manner that I've seen used by actors in afternoon black and white war-films. His office always smells of camomile and hand-sanitiser, neither of which succeeds in stirring any memories. I enjoy the squeak of leather as I move on his couch. He encourages me to close my eyes and listen while he talks in a very monotone style. Today I am telling him about another of my dreams.

Why do you think that these dreams are not your own? he says.

Because I've never experienced anything like them, I say. *None of them. These must be the dreams of other people.*

He asks me to tell him what happened in this particular one.

I am hiding in a small dark space, I say. *Outside I can hear the screech of gulls. It's hot where I am. A breeze is blowing through a gap, creating a murmuring voice of escalating madness. If you listen closely you can make out words. There's a rectangular gap, through which the blue sky is occasionally crossed by wheeling birds. A young boy's face suddenly obscures the blue. Eyes gleaming, I feel a desire to steal the light from them. He climbs in beside me, carefully lowering the door as he hides inside the confine of darkness. I sigh, but this time the words are lost in the chaos of his excited breath. From outside comes the sound of someone's voice, counting out loud.*

Coming - ready or not.

The breeze rustles the mountain of black plastic bags that are doing their best to obscure this discarded chest-freezer in which I lurk. It's a frantic sound, as if nature itself is trying to warn him. But the lid clicks shut firmly and stale darkness devours the light. The boy bangs the lid, kicks desperately at the walls of his white tomb. I embrace the heat of his body, holding him tight until he eventually stops squirming.

Professor Braten says that perhaps I was trapped in a confined space when I was young. I shrug, relishing the squeak of leather. The blinds at his window create slats of shadow on the wall opposite.

Who knows? I say.

Ⅱ

You might remember me from the newspaper reports in the days after the terrorist bombing—they referred to me as the *modern-day Kaspar Hauser* due to the mysterious past that we both shared. Google it if you're not familiar with the story. Personally I think that if it hadn't happened in Germany, I doubt anyone would have made the comparison—but that's journalists for you. Even in the ten months I've been back in England I've learned a fair bit about how reporters work.

According to the police files and witness statements, no one saw me at all before the explosion. I don't appear on any of the CCTV footage. I was carrying no identification when I was found in the rubble of the train station's central concourse. I had no wallet, although there were 58 Euros in my pocket. My clothes had been purchased from stores in the UK. There was no evidence of me even having bought a train ticket. It was as if the explosion had torn a hole in the world, through which I fell.

I regained consciousness on the 2nd December. By then, ISIS had claimed responsibility, and the whole world had stood in solidarity with the German people. Initially the mystery surrounding my presence in Germany had been viewed with some suspicion, but the CCTV footage and subsequent evidence made it quite clear who the actual perpetrators of the atrocity were.

I was an anomaly. I spoke English—*was* English as far as I knew—but everything else was a blank. I had no idea what I was doing in Nuremberg. No idea who I was. Still no idea. Medical experts gauged me to be between 32 and 35. I'm a male Caucasian, of fairly good physical health, with above average IQ. The condition of my hands suggest I was employed in an administrative role, unused to manual labour. I may have jogged in my spare time; perhaps I cycled.

I was wearing no jewellery. I am uncircumcised. I have no surgical scars or distinguishing features or tattoos. My fingerprints are not on any police database. The psychometric assessments I undertook have shown me to have marginally liberal views with no apparent bias towards any particular social class or ethnicity. I can drive a car, and I most probably learned in the UK. And I have a particular penchant for jazz music.

Ⅱ

Professor Braten likes to drop in the odd German word at opportune moments, especially those he seems most proud of—the ones used in English due to there being no real English equivalent.

Schadenfreude.

Zeitgeist.

Kaffeeklatsch.

Poltergeist.

This morning I'm listening to the beeps and mechanical gasps of the truck outside as the rubbish bins are emptied. It is a reassuringly robust sound. Professor Braten is telling me about how human personality is developed; how we are shaped by life experiences and how our minds become influenced by the viewpoints and emotions to which we are exposed. Unfortunately I've no evidence of any of that core framework so I have nothing upon which to base my feelings. It feels like I'm a sculpture, encased in a block of stone. Each day sees me chip away at the excess material to expose the real personality beneath. I'm learning new things about myself on a daily basis.

Professor Braten asks me if I'm still having the dreams.

Yes, I tell him. *Dreams about people dying, mostly.*

So do you still think they might be other people's dreams? His eyes reflect a bright rectangle from the morning sun pouring in through the window.

I do. It doesn't feel like me dreaming them. I add: *Why do you think they're always about death?*

He raises an eyebrow. *Maybe your subconscious can't believe that you survived the explosion so it's exploring the various aspects of death—imagining different scenarios.*

Maybe… I concede.

I tell him about my fear that I'm trapped in limbo, as if I'm waiting for an epiphany to strike, one that might shine light onto the real me.

Most people, he says, *who undergo a traumatic experience as you've done, come to view that moment as 'before' and 'after' because their lives are changed forever by what has happened. In your case you've no memory of 'before' so you're trying to piece together fragments from your own psyche. It's a little bit like trying to complete a jigsaw in the dark.*

It's very frustrating because I've no real way of knowing if my sessions with Professor Braten are doing me any good. All I *do* know is that the absolute terror that gripped me in the first days of my awakening seems to be dissipating—that overwhelming feeling that my memory-loss would return and I'd be plunged back into the fog of confusion.

He tells me he'll prescribe a short course of drugs to help with my dreams. I'm not sure whether to feel panic or relief.

Have you listened to those CDs? he asks.

I nod, even though I haven't yet had time. My apartment still feels alien, like it belongs to someone else and I'm just staying there temporarily. The CDs are stacked next to my music system, gathering dust. After I left the hospital, the NHS authorities helped relocate me to a furnished flat in sheltered housing, complete with intercom in case of emergency.

Professor Braten writes my prescription and I thank him and make my way out of his office. Outside I wait patiently while his receptionist books my session for the following week. As soon as she's finished she looks up at me with a smile and hands me my appointment card. *Didn't I see you at the museum on Saturday?*

I look at her, puzzled, faintly shaking my head. But I'm not quite sure. I'm not quite sure of anything. *I'm sorry, I think you must be mistaken.*

Really—at the one on Cavendish Street? I could've sworn it was you. She frowns, herself puzzled, confusion furrowing her brow, narrowing her eyes. *I thought you must have found yourself a job...*

I shrug and take my leave, uncertainty slowing my movement. Once I'm out on the street I have time to process her words. Instinctively I can dismiss her suggestion as erroneous. But there's a nagging doubt in the far recesses of my mind. How can I be sure that I *wasn't* at the museum on Saturday? I think back to my whereabouts at the weekend but, as is often the case, how can I be sure that my memories are nothing more than the dreams of others? I have a vague feeling that on Saturday I ate some lunch at a café in town, then browsed the antique market for an hour. But I'm as uncertain about that as I am about anything in my life.

I walk aimlessly for a while, considering the implications of the receptionist's words, not really comprehending the direction of my journey, when I realise I've reached the park on the outskirts of the suburbs. I see the hills rising gently behind the housing estate; the grey concrete and brown stone being replaced by the lush greens and patchwork fields. The juxtaposition feels like I'm moving from one specific location to another, this one a more organic, tranquil place. For twenty minutes or so I sit on the bench and watch a dog chasing a stick thrown by its owner, marvelling at the unquestioning devotion the animal displays each time it retrieves the stick. I am envious of the dog's ability to interact.

Eventually I realise that there is one way to solve my mind's conflict. Cavendish Street is but a fifteen minute walk away.

II

The first doctor that helped me—when I was transferred from Germany to London—seemed unwilling to go into much detail when discussing my anxiety. This may have been due to my reluctance to be hypnotised. He certainly appeared more focused on the physical aspects of my trauma than the mental ones. I think he considered my amnesia a temporary thing, something that would return if I left it well alone. He even displayed outward contempt at my theory that I was dreaming other people's dreams. Eventually I got fed up with the sessions and announced I had some vague idea that I was originally from Yorkshire—an entirely fabricated story—and so the NHS foundation transferred me to my present location in Sheffield.

It was here that I came under the care of Professor Braten. His nationality chimed with my instinct of synchronicity. It felt that I'd merely been passed from the left hand to the right. He showed far more willingness to engage in my wild theories, which in turn meant that I was receptive to the treatment he prescribed. Even though I still felt like I was floundering in darkness, at least it meant that there was someone there to guide my direction.

♊

There's a Perspex bus-stop on Cavendish Street, a short distance opposite the entrance to the museum. I shelter in it and observe the museum for a while. It's one of those modern buildings, very minimalist, acutely bland. All beige brickwork and reflective glass. For the next hour or so, a meagre array of visitors enters through the automatic doors. The adjacent car-park fills steadily, but more often than not the drivers just nip over the road to the shopping arcade rather than visiting the museum. Eventually I pluck up the courage to cross at the lights and stand awkwardly outside, trying to peer into the dim foyer through the glass doors. There's a woman seated behind a desk, chatting to a uniformed security guard standing nearby, occasionally answering the phone.

I feel terrified. I want to go inside but the thought of the woman recognising me arrests my movement. It would confirm my fear, that the reality I now think exists is just a façade; that my mind is interpreting the fugues I'm experiencing as dreams.

There's a coffee-shop further down the road, so I call in and take a leisurely amount of time drinking my latte, hoping to build up enough courage to return to the museum and ask the receptionist if she knows who I am. I convince myself that she's the answer to my questions.

Just as I'm leaving I see a male figure come out through the doors of the museum. He is carrying an armful of folders. I gape. It feels like reality is being torn from around me. He walks to the car park. I step tentatively along the pavement, staring at him as I close the distance, barely breathing, my body taut, fighting to stay in control. I can barely believe what I'm seeing. He looks *exactly* like me. Absolutely identical in fact—even his mannerisms and gait.

Thoughts begin to fire through my brain. Could this be my actual twin brother? The resemblance to me is uncanny. But then I feel a surge of dismay as I realise the coincidence of me coming to Sheffield to meet up with my own family member is fantastical, too far-fetched to be credible. Maybe a part of my subconscious knows that I am originally from the area, and when I suggested coming to Sheffield it wasn't as random as I thought?

He doesn't notice me. I watch him walk to a black Honda Civic parked in one of the designated staff bays and deposit the folders onto the back seat. He still doesn't notice me. I don't even feel conspicuous as I stand there. It's as if I have become invisible, like a ghost watching events from an ethereal plain.

II

I had borrowed a book from the library called *Past Lives—Stories of Reincarnation*, but it was really just about something called cryptomnesia, so—whilst very interesting—it didn't really shed any light onto my predicament.

Professor Braten had asked if the medication was suiting me and I'd told him it was. However I'd researched the drug on the internet and had decided to stop taking it because it was mainly used to treat schizophrenics and other related disorders.

I started to believe that he was trying to conceal from me the knowledge that I'd actually died in the explosion in Nuremberg, and that I was walking the earth in search of some real purpose, trapped in limbo between this world and the next. I wasn't always convinced that people could see me. My dreams were becoming darker and darker. The constant theme was death. It felt *premonitory*, inevitable, ungoverned. I started to forget how I looked. Every time I caught sight of my own reflection in a mirror or in a glass door I had to concentrate to remember who it was. The features of my face seemed alien and unfamiliar.

When I asked Professor Braten why my dreams were plagued by death, he turned the question back on me: *Why do* you *think so many of your dreams feature death?*

I shrugged. *Because I'm having the nightmares that other people usually have?*

I think you're struggling with the guilt of surviving the explosion, he says. *One Hundred and eleven people died that day. You're experiencing survivor guilt.*

That may be true. But perhaps I was a bad person *before* the terrorist attack. Maybe my absence of memory is my psyche's way of wiping the slate clean. Now—from here on in—I can be whoever I want to be. This is my chance to start again.

I don't have to feel governed by my past. Because I don't have one.

I don't need to feel influenced by my life's experience. Because I've lost all evidence of it.

Right now I can start inventing *me*.

♊

He locks his car and stands for a few moments checking his phone. On the street a car honks its horn and he glances up for a second before returning to the display. He's still unaware of my presence, standing transfixed approximately twenty feet away, watching him intently.

I am your ghost, I think to myself. *Do I dream your dreams?*

Presently he tucks his phone back into his pocket, glances at his watch and heads back into the museum.

I remain where I am, considering which direction I should allow my thoughts to proceed. Overhead, birds hurry across the sky. Behind me a bus hisses to a shuddering halt and allows passengers to disembark. The sour stench of diesel surrounds me.

The city continues to do its thing; the sights and sounds, the smells, the ever-revolving gears of progress. And here am I, snared in a state of stasis like an insect in a killing jar.

I linger. I endure the day. The October afternoon soon ushers in darkening clouds. I wait until the lights are on and shadows fill the streets. I go to the car-park and stand behind the Honda Civic, looking at the registration plate, my fingers touching the rear window where the *Princess On Board* card is affixed, only the cold thin glass separating it from me. Finger-marks pattern the grime around the lock of the boot. There is a book on the parcel-shelf: *The Very Hungry Caterpillar*. I walk to the front of the car. I peer in through the windscreen and notice a thick manila envelope on the passenger seat. I try to read the spines of the CDs stacked in a section of the dashboard but the only one I can make out is called *Bird – the Complete Charlie Parker.* I suddenly think of something, and return my attention to the manila envelope. There is a white address label visible, upside down, bearing the printed words *Mr W Wilson, 211 Fulwood Road, Dore, Sheffield, S17 3BP*. I murmur the address, as if sampling how the words feel in my mouth. My tongue and lips form the sounds and they suit my voice, my tone, the timbre, as if I were meant to say them.

I stand back and look at the car again, imagine him washing it on a Sunday morning, picturing him vacuuming the rear foot-well clean of raisins or sweet wrappers.

♊

I speak to Professor Braten about the story in the newspapers—the way they referred to me as Kaspar Hauser.

Does it bother you that they called you that? he asks.

Not really. I'd never heard of it before the papers brought it up. I smile mischievously. *Although it would be nice to find out I had royal blood.*

Professor Braten glances at me over the top of his glasses. *It's now commonly accepted that Hauser was a fake. That he fabricated the whole story. That he wasn't killed by some unknown stranger, and that he actually inflicted the fatal stab wound on himself.*

I feel like he has deflated me somewhat so I don't reply, just look at his bookcase as if I'm searching for a particular title.

Are the tablets I prescribed helping with your disassociation? He clicks the end of his pen to indicate he will begin to make notes.

I tell him they are. I tell him my memory loss is still there but the dreams have stopped and the sense of disassociation has eased. I tell him I'm thinking of getting a job.

I'm not sure you're ready for that, he says. *Might be worth continuing with these sessions until you feel a little more... clarity.*

I'm ready to join the real world. I try to hold a measure of insistence in my voice. I maintain eye contact until he glances down at his notepad. I can hear someone hurrying by, out in the corridor.

♊

In this dream I am squirming on a chair in a darkened theatre, watching the stage. The curtains twitch and I feel excitement and nerves fluttering in my chest. I know how nervous she will be. All those hours of rehearsal just seemed to increase the pressure, rather than easing it. But she knows what she has to do. It's all the rehearsal time that will now pay dividends because her auto-pilot will kick in and she'll do what she was meant to. There'll be no lines forgotten, no missed cues, no awkward phrasing or stumbling over her words. I smile broadly as the curtains slide open and she steps out onto the stage and into the spotlight.

Right at that moment I awake. I lie for a few moments while the cobwebs of the dream disintegrate and fall away, and it's only then that I hear the phone ringing. I sit up.

It's late afternoon. I can hear a quiz show playing on the TV in the other room. The phone continues to ring. I get up off the sofa and glance around, confused. It isn't the landline phone ringing and I don't own a mobile phone. But I can hear the ring tone somewhere in the kitchen. I stumble blindly in and almost slip as my socks struggle on the floor tiles. The ringing is persistent, startling.

I have a cutlery drawer beneath my hob and I yank it open. There, over to the left in the section reserved for larger knives, is a silver mobile phone. I can see that as well as ringing, it's vibrating in the shallow channel, causing a weird combination of metal-clang and plastic-buzzing. I pick it up and peer at the display. It has a picture of a smiling attractive brunette and the words RACHAEL CALLING.

Hello? My voice sounds alien, even to me. Perhaps it's because I'm anxious.

127

Will—it's just me. Can you pick up some spinach and dried pasta on your way home? The woman sounds breathy and in good spirits.

I'm sorry?

There is a pause then and I think she must have hung up but then she speaks again. *It's me. Is everything okay?*

Who's me?

There's very nearly a half-laugh. *Stop messing about, Will. Just get the stuff. I'll see you later, yeah? Don't be late tonight.* She gives the illusion of having taken control, but then to spoil the effect she adds, *Okay?*

Yep, no problem, I say. The call ends and I stare at the lock-screen of the phone. It's a photo of me sitting next to the same brunette from the earlier photo—Rachael? A girl, aged about four or five, sits on my knee. Behind us I can see the beach.

I feel disconnected, like I'm observing the action from somewhere remote.

It's much later when I suddenly look up from the sofa and notice the ten o'clock news is on. My body feels stiff; pins and needles ache my arm where I've been reclining. I glance around for the mobile phone but it's nowhere to be seen. I go into the kitchen but it isn't in the cutlery drawer either. It's difficult to know whether the phone call I took was just a dream. It certainly felt real but then many things feel real at the moment and yet I know a great deal of them are mere delusions.

Ⅱ

Mr W Wilson usually has his lunch around noon. Sometimes I've seen him eating it in the local deli; occasionally he fetches a sandwich from a shop on the corner and eats it back at the museum, presumably in some dusty room upstairs. One time I saw him eat it out in his car while he spoke at length on his phone.

I've watched him for nearly three weeks and I've been careful not to let him see me. The uncanny resemblance between us wouldn't fail to disturb him. I feel instinctively that he isn't my twin brother or any kind of family member or even someone who resembles me to a remarkable degree; the way he moves is just too similar to me—his mannerisms, his speech pattern, even the way his handwriting is formed is eerily identical to mine.

My initial thought that he was a family member has now given way to doubt. Not doubt about him being a family member but rather doubt that he's so similar to me. Maybe I'm projecting my own identity onto someone else as a way of explaining the enigma of my own identity.

211 Fulwood Road is a pleasant Victorian mid-terrace on a tree-lined street in a very nice area of the city. I've sat for several hours and watched him in an evening, noticing which lights go on at which times. This enables me to guess which room is which and helps me to build up a picture of his family's structure. He usually arrives home at 6pm and they eat their evening meal in a room directly behind the very comfortable front lounge, into which I can see via the huge bay-window that looks out onto the street. So far I've not been able to spot his wife, but his daughter is indeed the little girl I saw/imagined on the screen-lock of the phone. They usually bath her around 7pm. The light from the frosted window at the back tells me that. The small bedroom at the front of the house must be where his daughter sleeps because the faint glow is enough to suggest she uses a night-light. Then they usually draw the curtains and, I assume, spend their evenings watching television.

Most times they retire to bed between 11 and midnight. The front bedroom window indicates that one of them reads for around 15 minutes before they switch off and go to sleep.

I spend my time observing this routine, imagining the detail that goes on between that I can never be privy to.

♊

Professor Braten frowns when I ask him about the chances of one bumping into someone who's their absolute double.

Seeing people who you think look like you could be a facet of your condition. Maybe we ought to up your medication. He absently taps the top of his pen against a notepad on the desk.

It's just one person really, I say. *One particular person.*

He scratches his chin and raises an eyebrow and says one of those German words that he loves so much.

Doppelgänger.

He smiles at my puzzlement. *A doppelgänger,* he explains, *is a creature from folklore thought to be an omen, a harbinger of bad luck. Sometimes it's seen as a portent of death.*

I shrug. I can see he is trying to make light of my comment. He tells me he is going to try me on some different medication. I just nod. I squash the word I'm trying to remember—*his* word—into my mind, picturing the letters and the rhythm of how it sounds, all four syllables. The fact it's German makes me feel at a disadvantage, like it's something not just beyond the comprehension of my limited knowledge but also outside of the realm of my own culture.

II

So it comes to this.

This inevitability was always there. Maybe it's all part of the blueprint, together with my memory loss, the explosion, the months I've spent rehabilitating myself mentally. I seem to have come into the world as an anomaly but I'm not just going to accept the situation and let it play out like I have no choice in the matter.

I've researched the doppelgänger. If you believe the mythology, it means certain death for me. It means that I'm on borrowed time. Maybe this is, after all, nature's way of correcting the mistake of me not dying in Nuremberg.

I'm not going to play along.

I've thought long and hard about this. It all fits together—the reference to Kaspar Hauser and both his and my connection to Nuremberg. Here was a mysterious figure with a past shrouded in uncertainty, one who was allegedly stabbed to death by a stranger. Even the nationality of Professor Braten seems too coincidental. It appears that my state of limbo is about to reach its end.

But I'm ahead of the game. I've been withholding my medication so my mind is clear and analytical. I don't resemble the compliant sheep they want me to be.

Forty-five minutes later I'm standing in the bus-shelter opposite the museum, listening to rain drum on the Perspex roof, trying not to think that it is counting down the seconds I have left to live. Traffic swishes past, like languid whales in an ocean of grey. Lights burn in many of the windows. People hurry by, their faces concealed by umbrellas or hoods. I fight to ignore the distractions. Confusion tugs at my mind but I quell it by staring across at the museum.

What is Mr W Wilson doing up there in his dusty office? Is he plotting my downfall or does he simply not exist when I don't think about him; is he as lifeless as one of his own exhibits?

It's nearly time. The building adjacent to the museum is undergoing renovation. Scaffolding and polythene coating surround it, making it look like an insect cocooned within a temporary shell. I ponder what new building will emerge when the transformation is complete. I shelter beneath a canopy of industrial sheet, the metal struts of scaffolding rising above me like a series of spindly legs. I watch and I wait.

At the expected time, he comes out of the museum. He chats to the security guard for a moment at the door.

Just then I happen to glance down and spot a couple of discarded tools and cable-ties in the debris scattered around the base of the construction area. It feels like I was meant to see them. I bend down and pick up a screwdriver, wiping it on my jeans. Is this all part of a predestined event? It seems like my actions are not my own.

He finishes the conversation and waves vaguely, turning up the collar of his jacket as he steps out of the shelter of the building and enters the car-park. I make my move.

He has opened his car door and is just bending to climb in when he spots me. He recoils as if he has been shot. There is a grimace of surprise on his face. He stands frozen to the spot, his eyes wide. I stride up and open the passenger door and climb in.

There is a moment where I think he might be refusing to join me, but then he swings his body into the driver's seat and slams the door. He stares at me, taking in my appearance. His mouth is still agape. I never thought people actually did that in real life but here he is, really doing it. He stammers for a few moments, while coherent thought evades him.

Who are you? His voice sounds like mine, his face the carbon-copy of my own. I see the grey spots in his stubble match identical areas of my chin.

My own hands are trembling. *Drive.*

Where?

I shrug. *Anywhere. Just go.*

He switches on the engine and slowly drives out of the car park. I can see his movement is sluggish as he tries to compute what is happening. It's clear that he's instinctively heading home.

I feel terrified, unsure of what to do. He doesn't speak, just goes through the motion of driving. I want to ask him why he's not questioning how we're so similar but part of me is afraid to, because deep inside I think it might be because he's not real. Just a figment of my imagination.

We reach the ring-road and he takes the dual-carriageway, headed towards Dore. We pick up speed. Still he does not speak.

Where are we going? My voice sounds weak in the silence, even failing to compete with the sound of the engine and the swish of the windscreen wipers. I wonder if he's even heard me. Again, a little louder: *Where are we going?*

My house. He doesn't even look at me. *This is too weird.*

The word 'house' brings to mind H*auser* so I don't reply. All at once I realise I'm still holding the screwdriver. I look up at him and see the half-anxious-half-determined set of his face—*my face*—and I grip the handle of the screwdriver and drive the shaft deep into the side of his stomach.

He gasps, like a balloon about to deflate and peers down at himself, at the screwdriver sticking out of his body. At the black-red stain spreading across his

133

abdomen. A low wail escapes his mouth. He stares at me, incredulous.

All at once there is an almighty thud and we are wrenched sideways. My neck is jerked against the seatbelt and the meagre lights outside the car swirl and spin. A snowstorm of glittering glass explodes at me, scattering beads against my chest, into my hair, against my face. I can hear the loudest sound I have ever heard—a deafening roar of scraping metal—and it hurts my head. And then all I know is darkness and silence.

♊

For a time before I am fully awake, I'm aware of people speaking. They seem hazy, like voices in dreams. You hear it but don't understand what is being said. They could be speaking German for all I know. But then certain words bleed through into my consciousness and I know I'm slowly beginning to swim towards the light.

A car-crash on the Parkway.

No other vehicles involved.

Life-threatening injury.

Drifting in and out of consciousness.

Severe head trauma resulting in memory loss.

I can sense the presence of someone nearby so I struggle to open my eyes. She smiles, baring a wide set of tiny white teeth. *Daddy!* It is the little girl I saw on the phone-lock screen, presumably W Wilson's daughter. I offer back a weak smile and close my eyes just as a look of disappointment washes over her face.

It's okay, Hannah. Your dad is still coming round. This voice speaks from the other side.

I try to shift round. My sight is blurry but I can make out that I'm in a hospital room. There is a smell

134

of camomile and hand-sanitiser, but also an undercurrent of floor-polish, and I think of Professor Braten. My struggle to turn over is restricted by various wires and tubes that are coming out of me. I feel a hand on my forearm.

It's okay, Mr Wilson. Just take it steady. Rest for a while.

I can make out a figure through my half-closed eyes.

I'm Doctor Pradesh, Mr Wilson. You look much better than you did when you came in here. How are you feeling today?

I swallow audibly. There is a tightness around my waist and I glance down at a swathe of bandages that are attached to my stomach.

Just a puncture wound, sustained in the crash. It's healing very well. Nurse Carlisle is due to tend to the dressing shortly.

I try to talk. *What happened? What—how did—what happened?*

You ran off the road. It was raining and your car came over the embankment. You ended up on the roof.

I try to turn my neck and glance around the room but the pain halts my progress. My neck aches, my head feels sore. I have pins and needles in my right leg. *Where was I... where was I going?*

You were just driving home from work. You lost control and skidded in the rain.

I suddenly feel scared. I think about my house and Professor Braten and my therapy. I wonder if anyone has watered my plants.

Will?

A face comes into view. It's the brunette from the phone I found in my apartment. She looks apprehensive, her face etched with concern. Yet despite all that she is stunningly beautiful. Those

135

hazel eyes, the shining dark hair, her slender chin. She holds my hand. *How are you, darling?*

I nod my head once. *I'm fine. I'm fine.*

She smiles and it lights up her face. *The doctor says you've had a little bit of memory loss. He said it might take a while to come back. So you must rest up for a while. Then we'll take you home.*

I think about the little Victorian terrace and the bath-time routine and the comfortable lounge and the dining room through the back. I think about it and tears come into my eyes.

Can you remember much of what happened? Her voice is soft and appealing. She grips my hand, her warm fingers entwined around mine.

I shake my head slowly. *All I know is you and Hannah. I'm not sure of anything else.*

She smiles again, and this time it seems like a satisfied, reassured one. *Don't worry. We'll take care of you.* She bends and plants a soft moist kiss on my cheek. She smells beautiful. I watch her take the little girl by her hand and walk towards the door. She is slim and athletic.

Rachael.

She turns, smiling at the sound of my voice.

I love you.

I love you too, she says.

I watch her leave. In my head I think of my new name—Will Wilson—and decide it sounds like a superhero from a comic-book. I imagine being a father, being a husband, being someone's boss. I imagine sitting up in that dusty office at the museum. I lie in that hospital bed and think about what kind of man I'm going to be. The slate is blank. But it's going to be fun finding out.

Hold My Hand And I'll Take You There

Ralph Robert Moore

The end of the world began when Noah came in one day from the backyard, shuffling over to his mother at the stove, head bent, saying he didn't want to plant any more snapdragons in his garden. He was tired.

The fall before, Noah spent quiet afternoons out in the section of the backyard designated as his garden, little body kneeling down in the dirt, serious look on his face, big metal spade in his right hand, digging brown holes. Lowering the beige roots of depotted petunias and snapdragons into the ground. Small hands parenthesizing the pile of evacuated dirt, escorting it back to the hole, filling in the curved sides, forming a small berm around each planting. In the early spring, what he put in the ground, and watered and watched over, bloomed wild colors, yellow, purple, red. His four foot height, witnessing the secrets in the soil. If it can grow, it might grow. He stood by the wide spread of that rainbow in his baggy pants, hands by his sides, grinning. Because his parents were proud of him. Camera to their right eye, taking pictures.

"Did you sleep okay last night? Is that why you're tired?"

Noah shrugged, his mother glancing back at the stove. To make sure nothing was burning.

"You don't still think there's a monster in your closet, right? Or that it snuck under your bed when your dad pulled all your soccer gear out of the closet to show you it was safe?"

Shook his dark-haired head. "Can I lie down?"

♊

"Why are your pajamas so wet?"

Noah, sitting at his customary place at the round breakfast nook table, feeling embarrassed. Avoided eye contact with his mom. "I didn't pee in my pajamas."

His dad, sitting next to him, cupped Noah's thin shoulder. "No one's saying that, buddy." Lifted his fingers off the shoulder of his son's pajamas, looking at the undersides of his fingers. "Were you sweating a lot during the night?"

Noah picked at his favorite breakfast, scrambled eggs and bacon, moving the yellow and red around on his plate, small face going into defense mode. "Maybe a little bit, I guess."

♊

Dr. Crane-Wyling sat in a chair next to where Noah stood bare-legged in his paper examination gown. Blonde hair pulled in a bun behind her head, breathing heavily through her nostrils, she traced her right index finger down Noah's test results. Raised her thin face, glanced at both parents. "Well, Noah does have an elevated temperature, and his body weight's down ten pounds. Which is unusual." She winked at the self-conscious boy. "Do you get dizzy, Noah?"

"No, Doctor."

"Never?"

Noah, looking up at the white ceiling. "Maybe once or twice."

"Okay. Mind if I ask you some more questions?"

His embarrassment. "No, of course not."

Eyebrows arching. "Do you have any bruises?"

"I guess."

"He has a bruise on his back from when he fell off a rocking horse outside a supermarket, and that's been there for maybe a month."

"Good to know. Any bleeding, Noah? Like nose bleeds, or any other type of bleeding?"

"Not really."

"He has had nose bleeds though. Remember, buddy? Sunday after we grilled some chicken in the backyard?"

"Just a few more questions, then you can go back home with your mom and dad. When you brush your teeth, do your gums bleed?"

"I'm not sure."

"Well, when you spit out your toothpaste, is it white, or pink?"

"I guess maybe sometimes it's pink."

Her right hand beckoned for Noah to stand closer to where she was seated. Head averted, she dug her fingers into Noah's underarms. His groin, causing Noah to blush, especially since his parents were right there. Sides of his neck. Felt around Noah's lower ribs. "I notice that even though your weight has dropped, your stomach's a bit swollen."

Noah, mortified that a lady had touched him down there, didn't know what to say, so he said nothing.

Her calm voice. "So there is some enlargement of Noah's lymph nodes, and I do feel an enlargement of his organs by his lower ribs. You know, I think it might just benefit us to run some additional blood tests on this young man, just to see what we find. Grace can do that."

♊

"When we get to the Baskin-Robbins, can I get three different ice cream scoops, instead of just two?"

His dad, driving, glanced at his mom in the front seat. "You know, why not?"

His mom turned around in her seat belt so she could see Noah sitting by himself in the back seat. "Do you know what the third ice cream flavor will be?"

Noah took his eyes from the side window. All these people on the sidewalks he didn't know. "I want to wait until we get to the store to decide."

His dad looking in the rearview mirror. "Hey buddy, before we go to Baskin-Robbins, the three of us are going to just swing by the medical building for a few minutes. Okay?"

Noah sat up straight in the back seat. Alert. "Why are we doing that?"

"Remember that blood sample they took last week? They've run it through a whole bunch of tests, and today they're going to tell us what they found. That's a good thing, right?"

His mom reached behind her car seat, touched his small knee. "But you probably won't have to get undressed this time. And there probably won't be any more needles."

Once they were in the new examination room, Noah put his palms on his knees, staring down at the floor.

"Ten minutes from now we'll be in the ice cream shop, buddy."

"Am I going to have to come back here still another time?"

"Probably not!"

Rapid knock on the door.

Only this time, when it opened, it wasn't Dr. Crane-Wyling. It was a short, older man with gray and black hair, wearing a white coat. He reached down to shake both parents' hands from where they were sitting, surprised.

The man took a seat on the rolling stool in the room. "I'm Dr. Paul Zyzksewlowski." Wry twist of his eyebrows. "I know that's hard to remember how to pronounce. Most patients just call me Dr. Paul." Both parents rearranged themselves in their chairs, glancing at each other. "And I'm guessing this young man here is Noah. Am I right?"

Noah looked scared.

"Dr. Crane-Wyling, once she got the blood test results, asked me to take over Noah's case with regards to this current issue. Dr. Crane-Wyling will still handle all of Noah's other pediatric needs. So! I understand you've been getting kind of tired lately, Noah, and you've had some night sweats, bleeding and bruising incidents, some swollen lymph glands, and swelling in your upper abdomen." He opened the manila file in his lap, which was evidently Noah's blood test results. Smiled at the parents. "Give me a minute." His eyes went down the results. Flipped the stapled page to review the results on the second page.

Spread his black shoes apart on the floor. "Okay. Let's start by me feeling how swollen those lymph nodes are, okay, Noah?"

Ten minutes later, Noah down to his white underpants at that point, red-faced and upset, Dr. Paul told him he could get dressed again. Blue eyes going from mother to father. "So…Is this a conversation where we want Noah to be present, or is this a good time for him to go to the children's waiting room, where we have a lot of coloring books?"

The father looked unhappy. "How…"

"This is a mystery we have to solve. We use diagnostic tests, such as the blood work we did, plus a number of other medical procedures, to locate all the clues. Then those clues help us solve the mystery. Do you like mysteries, Noah?"

"No."

"The blood test results show that Noah is not producing red blood cells the way we would expect in a healthy eight year old."

"Noah's seven."

"Okay." Apology expressed as a duck of the head. "But, the same concern applies. A failure to produce red blood cells can indicate an inability to create lymphocytes." Dr. Paul smiled at the parents' confusion. "Lymphocytes are created in the bone marrow." Some of the hope in Mr. Wright's face went out. "Lymphocytes fight infections. When we see a reduction in the number of healthy lymphocytes in a patient's circulatory system, that can indicate the cells that would normally mature into healthy lymphocytes stall out once they reach the immature state. Immature cells are known as lymphoblasts."

Noah's dad shifted in his chair. "So what are you saying?"

"Lymphoblasts prevent normal red blood cells from forming. And white blood cells, and blood platelets." Dr. Paul looked at a wall. "That often indicates leukemia." He said nothing more.

Noah's mom touched her mouth. "You hear about leukemia, but I don't really know what..."

"Leukemia happens when normal blood cells change from the way they're supposed to be, and start growing uncontrollably. It's known as acute lymphoblastic leukemia. We call it ALL."

"Is it serious? Is there a pill Noah needs to be taking?"

Dr. Paul again ducked his head. In a determinedly conversational tone he said, "ALL is the most common form of childhood cancer."

Ⅱ

The door to the examination room creaked open.

Matilda, one of the oncology nurses, poked her long-haired head in. "Is that my favorite patient?"

Noah grinned shyly.

Matilda sashayed into the small room, one hand behind her back. Rubbed the top of Noah's bald head. "How you doing, Tiger?"

Noah inclined his head to the left. "I guess I'm doing okay."

Wink to the father. "You're not just doing okay. Because…today you're a hero!"

From behind her back, she swung her hidden hand forward. It held a brightly colored necklace. Noah's eyes widened.

Playful pulled punch to his shoulder. "That's right, mister! Today you've earned another Hero's Necklace! Wow, that makes, let's see." Index finger air-counting the other necklaces around Noah's frail neck. "Five! Hero's Necklaces!" She slid her eyes flirtatiously at Noah. "May I do the honors, Sir?"

Noah sat up even higher at the edge of the examination table, hollow cheeks, puppy dog eyes on Matilda. "Sure!"

When Matilda stepped in front of Noah to lower the latest honor, blocking his view, his dad quickly raised his right thumb and index finger to his eyes, blotting tears.

"Well, look at you, mister! What do you think, dad?"

"I'm so proud of you son. You earned it."

"Gosh."

"Is mom not here today?"

Mom's home sleeping off her hangover, and the big fight she and dad got into last night, shouting in whispers, so as not to alarm Noah. These past few months had been rough on her. "Jen came down with some kind of stomach flu. She wanted to be here, but

143

I told her to stay home and rest. She's going to be so thrilled, though. Five Hero Necklaces!"

"There's a lot of that going around." Unexpectedly, Matilda looked right into the dad's eyes. He saw her frozen stare, the extraordinary pain in her blue eyes. Swinging back to Noah. "Well, okay Mr. Hero. Today, you're going to see your old pal Dr. Emerson again, but guess what? We're gonna have a guest star, too! Dr. Sapir."

"Who's he, Matilda?"

She put her hands on her white uniformed hips. "Well, he's just about one of the smartest guys I ever met, outside of you! That's who he is!"

Noah's dad smiled, because you had to smile a lot around Noah at this point. "What's Dr. Sapir's specialty?"

"Since we put Noah in clinical trials he's had quite a few chemo sessions, but in his case the ALL has been, you now, kind of aggressive, so this is a good time to pull out our next weapon, which is radiation therapy. The type of therapy Noah will be receiving—" Grin at the little boy sitting on the edge of the examination table— "Is called external-beam radiation therapy. And that's the most common type of radiation therapy, by the way. Like we discussed Monday, our latest diagnostics show the ALL has spread to Noah's spinal fluid, and we want to stop it before it spreads to his brain or the naughty parts." Wink at Noah.

A knock on the examination room door. Two men entering, both in white jackets. Noah's dad glanced at Matilda, who had retreated to the small stainless steel hand-washing sink, now cast in a supporting role. He has just one child with cancer. How does she bear the weight of all the dozens and dozens of scared kids she has to cheer up each week?

144

II

The frustrations he had to go through as a child—disappointing lab results, lying awake in bed late into the night for yet another surgery scheduled for the following morning—probably gave Noah the strength he needed later in life, dealing with Audrey.

As a child, she seemed cheerful. Skinny, enthusiastic, the adult eyes of certain girls. Got along well with the neighborhood kids, taking turns on the swings in the child-shouting dusk of suburban backyards. Her high-ceilinged bedroom pink, tidy. Lone sneaker, lying on its laced side, on the white carpet in front of her bed. The usual wall posters. Going on at dinner, mixing her mashed potatoes with her peas, about her different bracelets, world peace. The quiet mom and daughter moments, sitting together on the edge of Audrey's bed, mom's calm right palm stroking her crown, talking about books, boys. Parent-teacher meetings always left the Plathers feeling proud of their only child as they walked back to the dark parking lot. In high school, at the graduation ceremony, it was their daughter who walked across the outdoor stage to the microphone to give the valedictorian speech. It was titled, *The Eternal Baton*:

"Wrinkled hands reach down to young hands. And what those wrinkled hands place in our young hands is Legacy. It is now our turn to carry that Legacy forward, out into the world, making it an even better place for the next generation of young hands reaching up to our ageing hands, as they seize The Eternal Baton."

One afternoon, a week before she left for college, she came downstairs for breakfast with her blouse on backwards. Buttons down her back. Mr. Plather, standing by the round kitchen table where Audrey

145

sat, sipped his coffee. Smirked. "Is this a, What's wrong with this picture practical joke?"

Audrey looked up at him, puzzled.

"Your blouse. You put it on backwards."

Looking down at her blouse. Not raising her eyes. Blush on her cheeks. Without a word, running back up the stairs.

Just before Thanksgiving break, Audrey away at college, her pink bedroom empty and silent, shadows, both parents planned an extra special holiday visit for their daughter. Goose instead of turkey, oyster stuffing, homemade cranberry and orange jelly. Mrs. Plather researching recipes on the Internet. The two of them feeling older, but in a good way, like gray hair can sometimes be flattering, speculating over coffee whether or not she'd bring a guest. Probably a girl? Maybe a nervous boy? And what would they do then? But the excitement of it. Our little girl is growing up. Mr. Plather took a call in his home office on a late Tuesday night, while he was arranging his cloisonné collection. Put down his magnifying glass, lowering lens enlarging the grain of his green blotter.

He made the long highway drive by himself. Radio on, chewing pepsin gum the whole way. Once Audrey was back home, her mother could quietly find out what went wrong. But getting their girl out of the mental institution? Back to their family home? That's what a father did.

Given the Plather's wealth, he had gotten used to a deference when dealing with others. But there was none of that at the psychiatric hospital. The staff were indifferent to what he wanted. Heavy-set woman. "Sit in that chair. We'll come for you when she's finished with her latest counselling session. But only for a brief visit. She's still under observation."

"I'd like to participate in her session."

Hands on hips. Eyeglasses tilting down. "Did you not hear me?"

He checked into a nearby motel. Big sign on metal stilts at the front of the parking lot, by the road. The in-room coffee service tasted terrible. Visited her every day. White hospital gown, white bandages on her wrists.

At first her parents thought she'd only stay home a few days, just to make sure she was okay, then go back to college, but lying down all day in her darkened bedroom stretched to a week, then the next week, the next month. Mr. Plather found a psychiatrist who was supposed to be especially good at working with troubled teenage girls. He interviewed the man first, to get a take on him. Young, with a goatee Mr. Plather wasn't too sure about, it seemed to him to suggest affectation, but otherwise he seemed intelligent. Drove Audrey to the thrice-weekly sessions, waiting down in the parking lot in his car each hour. After a while, Audrey begged him not to have to go back to the psychiatrist. Good, he thought. Maybe Dr. Crowther is making progress. After one particularly rough breakfast, toast flung onto the kitchen floor, her father insisting she was going to her appointment that day, his daughter trying to get back upstairs to her bedroom, she fell down on the carpeted steps, looking up at his grabbing hands, hysterical. "He's fucking me, Daddy! He fucks me every time you march me in there, while you're down in your car!"

He brought a criminal lawsuit against the psychiatrist, which was dismissed for lack of evidence, then a civil suit, also dismissed. In the civil suit the psychiatrist counter-sued for defamation of character, and was awarded three thousand dollars. They got her a job at a local McDonalds, still living at home so they could keep an eye on her. She lost the job in less than a month, because she would be too depressed to show up for work.

She rarely left the house. She rarely left her room. She rarely left her bed.

Her mother would bring soup upstairs. But the spoon barely made it past her sad lips. Her anguished eyes, thin shoulders hiding under the blue blankets. Scared voice. "There's a mushroom in my brain, and it keeps crawling around in there, from one ear to the other ear." Eyes melting, hot, helpless tears.

Five years passed.

Audrey working at a veterinarian's office in a small town twenty minutes from her parents' home, grooming pets. Dogs were easier than cats. Makes sense. Her father had given the vet a loan to help him open up his own practice. She was driving down the main street of the town towards a take-out hot wings place where she ate lunch each day. Lost in her own worries, not listening to the car radio, when she broad-sided. A car up ahead of her, turning left.

Put her car in reverse, frightened face. Backed her front fender away from the big dent in the driver's side door of the car she hit. Twisting the steering wheel to maneuver around the accident, to the hot wings place.

The driver's side door of the car she hit swung open, hanging off its curled hinges. A tall man stepped out. "Hey!"

They had their first date two nights later, at Ricardo's Ristorante in her hometown.

She wore her little black dress, first time it had been out of the closet in years.

She was nervous. Looking around at the other quiet diners, trying to hide. Black-framed eyeglasses, because she had finally admitted she was near-sighted. The waitress dropped off their menus, taking their drink orders.

Noah had grown into a dark-haired, broad shouldered man. He smiled at her. "I pass by this place a lot, but I've never eaten here before. What's good?"

Tense, she shook her head. "I haven't eaten here."

"Oh! Since you suggested it, I thought…"

Angry eyes. "What is this, the third degree?" Turned her head to one side. He liked her profile. Not pretty, her nose was too prominent for that, but almost beautiful. Muttering to herself. "This is not going to work out."

"No, that's fine. I mean, I guess I just misunderstood. It'll be an adventure for both of us."

The waitress returned with their drinks. Raised her blonde eyebrows. Probably a college kid. Open face, good looks. "My name's Marcie. Do you know what you want?"

Audrey rolled her dark eyes. "We don't need to know your name."

Marcie, smile faltering. Flickering back into place. Almost. Showed Audrey her empty right palm. "I'm sorry. Management wants us to introduce ourselves. What would you like?"

Noah, who had been studying the menu, not really following what was going on, looked up. "This is my first time here. What do you recommend?"

"Well, if you like seafood—"

Audrey's furious voice. "You want to fuck her?"

That took a moment to register on Noah's face.

"Is that the kind of guy you are? You flirt with another girl right in front of me? Because you think she's prettier than me? Younger than me? What am I supposed to do? Just take it? Sit here obediently while she sucks your cock?" She threw her drink at Noah's shirt.

Ⅱ

"Don't take me home! If you take me home, I'm going to jump out my bedroom window. And that'll be on you. On your soul."

Noah steered his rental car to the left, getting up on the highway. Glanced over at Audrey in the passenger seat, grinding her teeth.

"Where are you taking me? I can't go home! Not this early. It'd kill my parents."

Cars passing by on both sides, metal roofs illuminated by the tall highway lights. "I can take you back to my place. We can order some pizza."

She looked in all the rooms of his apartment, even the closets. Under his bed.

Noah fixed her a drink. Gestured at his shirt, pants. "I'm going to take a quick shower. Get this booze off me. Then we'll order a pizza." Turned on the TV for her. Handed her the remote.

"Where's your longest knife?"

He stopped by his bedroom's doorway. "Why do you want to know that?"

"For the pizza!"

His embarrassment for her. "It's pre-sliced." Wanted to add, but figured it'd be a bad idea with her, How long's it been since you had pizza? Because you never know.

"What if they forget? We're going to let it get cold while we hunt for a knife? Ugh!"

Inside the master bedroom's bathroom, he got out of his clothes. Twisted the taps in the shower on. Left palm facing up, reaching inside the cubicle, to test the temperature. The bathroom door opened. Audrey staring in at his nakedness.

"I just need a couple of minutes to rinse off. I'm not going to wash my hair."

Got under the shower. Warm water washing down the sides of his face. Drive her home? Call her parents? Order and eat the pizza, then drive her home? Let her have the leftover slices?

The shower door opened out, cold air.

Audrey, long-haired, looking at his naked body.

"Do you want to take off your dress and come in her with me? Wash each other?"

Her outrage. "I showered before you picked me up!"

"Okay. I'm going to shut the shower door, because I'm getting a lot of cold air in here." Swung its glass against the metal frame.

Bent over, soaping his now erect cock, heard the shower door swing open.

"Audrey? What do you want?"

Long brown hair parted in the center of her scalp. "I'm hungry!"

He twisted off the taps. Stepped out of the shower cubicle, naked and dripping.

Looked around for his white bath towel.

Not here.

Audrey was lying on his bed. On her back. Nude. One thin bare knee drawn up. Proud of the shapely profile of her right thigh.

Glanced at his tall cock. Rolled onto her hip, facing him. Legs spreading, showing him her cunt. "Look how my pubic hair matches your pubic hair. We were meant to be together."

After kissing, after fingers moving between each other's legs, moans, groans, he slid his body on hers, belly to belly.

She stared up at him, smirking. "On? Or off?"

"On or off what?"

"The glasses. Some guys like to fuck girls while they're wearing their eyeglasses."

"Oh. On."

Her look of triumph, soft thighs closing around him, long muscles flexing, holding him in place.

Afterwards, after three orgasms in fact, Noah drained, Audrey hopped out of his bed. "I'm going to take a shower."

Too tired to look for the TV remote. "Okay."

Hiss of the shower. Her starting to sing, and actually her voice was quite musical.

A scream.

She banged into his bedroom, naked, soapy, furious. Waving the face cloth in her right hand. "What the fuck is this?"

"What?"

"This!"

Brought it over to him. Held it out. Dripping white bubbles. Monogram on one side. Three pink letters. "That was…it belonged to a former girlfriend. She left some of her stuff here. I'm sorry. Where did you find it?"

She used it to slap him across his face. "I'm going to rub my crotch with your ex-girlfriend's initials? Really, Noah? Burn it. Burn it right now!"

"It's too wet to burn. Let me put it in the dryer, and—"

Thin shoulders hunching up, hands rising to her temples. In the highest, loudest voice he had ever heard: "Burn it! Burn the fucking thing! Burn it!"

♊

The radiation therapy wasn't enough.

Noah's latest doctor, Dr. Nordent, a grown man sitting on a stool, read his chart, flipping page after page impatiently, while Noah and his dad waited in chairs. At one point, Noah looked at his dad. His dad brightened. Winked.

Dr. Nordent closed the file, laid it on his lap. "Well. There's a lot here in the test results to be cautiously optimistic about. So, good news. I do have

152

to agree with Dr. Plinkett that we have to proceed with a stem cell transplant."

Noah's dad rubbing his palms against the tops of his thighs. "I checked with my insurance, and they don't cover that procedure. So, what would it cost me? We're going to do it, no matter what, but I just need to know so I can plan for it."

Dr. Nordent grinned good-naturedly. Brought his right fingertips up his white-jacketed chest. "I'm not the billing office. So you'd have to check with them. But, ballpark, don't quote me, since it would have to be an allogeneic transplant, and given that costs have been coming down, since a lot of the work associated with the transplant can now be done outpatient, you're probably looking at somewhere between one hundred and fifty thousand dollars and two hundred thousand dollars."

His dad nodded. Cleared his throat. "And how much of that would I need to pay up front?"

Dr. Nordent closed his eyes, opened them. "You'd have to check with the billing office."

And the long wait started, to find a donor. If Noah had a brother or sister, they probably would have made an ideal donor. But he had no siblings. His dad was tested, and his dad contacted Noah's mom to have her tested, but neither were a good match.

Noah's hair was growing back. His appetite had returned. Some of the gauntness went out of his face. Every night, at the end of the day, he and his father would kneel by the side of Noah's bed, and pray that a donor would be found.

The prayers helped. But Noah would still end each evening by himself, in his bed, lying on his back, looking up at the car headlights sweeping across his ceiling. A lot to ask of anyone. A lot to ask of a little boy.

Noah returned to school. Some of his fellow classmates tied blue ribbons to their back packs in support. Others started calling him "Cancer Kid."

He walked home from school one day with Julie, this girl he was starting to hang out with, thinking about inviting her to have dinner with them, and his dad was sitting at their kitchen table, a stack of papers and a calculator in front of his big hands. His dad had been drinking. His eyes were wet. "They found a donor, son." His dad's face crumpled.

Ⅱ

"I'm going to be the first to say it. Audrey is not an easy person to get along with." Her dad's watery eyes, sitting behind his desk in his home office. Waiting for Noah's response from his visitor's seat at the front of the desk.

"You know, I don't disagree with you."

Distant sound of Audrey and her mother, setting the table, getting food out of the oven.

"She can be a real handful."

"I love her, Mr. Plathers."

Reached for his Manhattan. Avoiding Noah's eyes. Someone dealt a great poker hand. Look at all that royalty. "I believe you. I do."

Noah's helplessness. "I don't know why."

"Sure."

"But I just look at her, at her…confusion?"

"Okay."

"And I just feel so much for her. I want to be there for her. Find a way to make her happy. Because I think she can be happy. I had a difficult childhood."

"She told me. My God. So much for a kid to have to work through."

"And I don't know, I think—corny as this sounds—maybe part of the reason why I healed,

154

eventually, was that someday I could help Audrey heal."

Her dad couldn't speak. His old hand reached out across the desk top, clasped the top of Noah's hand.

"Boys? Come and get it!"

♊

Noah switched to speaker phone so he could change from his pajamas into street clothes and hunt down his car keys, wallet, while he spoke. "So is she stable?" While he thought of it, he wrote down the case administrator's name on the back of his left hand, so he could ask for her once he got to the emergency room.

"She's lost some blood, but I've seen worse. She's a common blood type, so that's not an issue. We're going to keep her overnight, but you can visit her, and in fact it would be good for her if you did. Then tomorrow we have to discharge her to a psychiatric facility. State law, with a suicide attempt. But her stay overnight here counts towards the seventy-two hour observation requirement."

The nurse at the facility lead Noah to the common area, a large room with a TV mounted high up on the wall at either end. Lots of windows along the east wall. He saw her sitting by herself in an easy chair by one of the windows, and wanted to cry. But didn't.

"Hey, sweetie."

Her forlorn face rotated up, some of the sorrow going out of it once she recognized him. Raised halfway up out of her chair, clinging to him like a child. Shivering. Trying to hide in his strength.

He petted the top of her head, nose buried in her hair, smelling the shampoo she used when she was in their home, and life was normal.

"You have to get me out of here!" Hollow eyes.

"I can't today. The law is, you have to stay here tonight, and tomorrow night. But then I'll pick you up, and we'll go back home. And everything will be all right again."

Her tears, as she collapsed against him. "I can't stay here! I won't survive."

"You will. Just like the last time. Then we'll go home, have a good night's sleep, and in the morning I'll fix you breakfast in bed. Anything you want."

II

"I'm right here!"

Dr. Sapherson rested his elbows on the arms of his chair, fingers interlaced in front of his stomach. "I apologize for talking about you in the third person, Audrey. But I need to bring your husband up to speed. Plus, I did want to see firsthand how the two of you interact."

Her dark-eyed defiance. "We interact just fine."

"You know, you actually do. I can see you draw a lot of strength from Noah, and I can also see how he's there to provide that strength to you. You're quite fortunate. Often, the spouse or significant other, over time, will draw away emotionally. Noah, you asked about where we go from here, and I'd like to just take a moment to review the approaches we've tried up to this point."

Audrey squeezed Noah's hand even harder, the two of them sitting side by side at the front of Dr. Sapherson's desk. Noah squeezed back.

Dr. Sapherson, observing, scribbled a note. "Here's our challenge. The longer a patient's depression continues, the harder it is to treat. Audrey's depression first manifested when she was eighteen? And now she's thirty-nine? That's twenty-one years of treatment-resistant depression. We've

156

established there are no thyroid-related causes, and our experiments with different SSRI's, SNRI's, and older classes of antidepressants such as tricyclics, tetracyclics, dopaminergics and MAO inhibiters just haven't proved fruitful. So I think we're ready to move on to ECT."

Noah, with his free hand, rubbed the bridge of his nose. "And that's electroconvulsive therapy?"

His wife squeezed his hand extra hard. "I don't want to do that. Seriously, Noah. Don't make me go through that. Please, honey."

Dr. Sapherson grinned. "It has a bad rep." Spread his hands apart. "Conceded. But it does often get remarkable results."

Desperate hand squeeze. "Honey? No. Don't listen to him. Please. For me. Please."

II

He wasn't allowed to be present during the ECT treatments. Only saw her afterwards, in the recovery room, her poor confused face slack, frightened eyes seeking for him, finding him, anchoring to him as he moved around her gurney.

As terrible as the treatments were, jerking her spine off the gurney, flattening her face, they did clear away some of the confusion. She'd stay bedbound a few days afterwards, babbling, but then a clarity would twang back into her eyes. He'd drive her home from the institute, and they'd always stop at a McDonalds on the way home, going through the drive-through, ordering fish fillet sandwiches and French fries, which they'd eat in bed once they were back in their apartment, Audrey ripping off the saw-toothed tops of the ketchup packets with renewed optimism.

It's going to work this time.

157

♊

Frederick, the new case manager, slipped the noose of another Hero's Necklace around Noah's thin neck. Smiled at the camera.

The interviewer leaned towards Noah, sitting frail in his wheelchair. "So, are you ready to win this war against cancer, Noah?"

Big eyes, staring at her. "It's really not a war. It's a prayer against cancer."

"And cut!"

"You're a star!"

His dad clapped Noah on his back, but gently.

Noah shy. "I just felt like maybe it might help other kids going through cancer treatment."

The local TV morning news anchor finished her discussion with the producer of the piece, walked back down the hospital corridor to be with Noah and his father. Latina, short black hair, slim. "You've got a real hero here!"

"Better believe I know it."

"We'll air the interview tomorrow morning." She bent forward, hands on her knees, smiling into Noah's eyes. "We're all praying for you, Noah." Gave him a private wink. "Especially Sylvia, the meteorologist." Noah blushed. "I told her what a fan you are. I'll burn a copy of your segment, and give it to your dad. You can watch it once you're back home, recovering from your surgery."

Once Noah was rolled into pre-op, his dad excused himself to make another call out in the corridor. Trying to get hold of his ex-wife, to see if she could come down to the hospital for moral support.

A nurse rolled another kid in a wheelchair into the pre-op room. Older than Noah. Bigger.

158

The kid looked at Noah's Hero's Necklaces, snorting. "Only girls wear necklaces."

Noah's feelings weren't hurt, because even at his young age, he knew the other boy was jealous of all Noah's necklaces. And he hoped the boy stayed jealous, that he never wound up with as many necklaces as Noah had, because each necklace represented pain, disappointment, fear. Noah was one of those rare kids, and too often it's only kids, who don't want anyone else to suffer as much as they do.

Noah's dad parked in his usual spot the next morning, his approach to the hospital's glass front doors causing them to automatically slide open, passing through the large, crowded lobby of anxious clusters, patients' family and friends, to the bank of elevators at the back. Bits of grass blades on the cuffs of his trousers. The lawn had been getting high; he figured he might as well mow it now, get it out of the way so he could stay by Noah's side once he was back home.

As he got off on the seventh floor, a clown holding balloons, face sad, fussing with the white collar of his costume. The clown looked up, saw Noah's dad staring at him.

His dad, embarrassed at getting caught. "When do you get in character?" The first thing that popped into his head. Hoped it didn't sound judgmental.

He could see it was a young guy behind the white and red makeup. Probably a college kid trying to make some extra money. Nothing wrong with that. "Usually just outside the hospital room's doorway. Sometimes, just inside the doorway."

"Makes sense." The two men nodded at each other. Strangers talking for a moment in a hospital who would never see each other again. Happens a lot.

Serena wasn't on duty at the nurse's station, but he recognized Jane. "How's our hero doing?"

159

She held up a forefinger. Pushed down a button. "Dr. Stratton to station. Dr. Stratton to station."

Dr. Stratton came out of one of the white corridor's doorways, recognizing Noah's dad. "Let's go in here."

Led him into a tiny office. Holding a bundle of reports in his right hand. Didn't sit down. "Noah unfortunately didn't make it through the night."

Noah's dad lost his smile.

"I am so sorry. He fought really hard, but just about twenty minutes ago, while he was in recovery, a blood clot formed and traveled to his brain before we could prevent it. I'm aware nothing is going to be a consolation to you at this point, but later on you might appreciate knowing he died almost instantaneously, with probably very little pain. Just a flash of light, and then he was taken from us."

II

"How do you like my hair?"

Audrey posed in their apartment's living room for Noah, delighted expression on her face.

She had cut it short. No more long dark hair parted in the middle of her scalp. Now it ended at her shoulders, neatly brushed, bangs across the high forehead. She was even more beautiful than before. You saw the hollows of her cheeks, the darkness under her eyes.

Noah stood back. "Wow. Well, I think it looks fantastic."

She nodded happily. "I thought if my hair was more orderly, maybe I'd think clearer thoughts." Peered at herself in the mirror over the sofa. "And I think it makes my crow's feet look less noticeable."

He put a hand on the back of his wife's shoulder. "You don't have crow's feet."

"Yeah." One of those 'yeahs' that are slightly loud, like the person knows the other has finished his sentence, but they're distracted.

Worriedly studying her image in the mirror. "I don't know. Maybe they're still too visible."

He didn't dare suggest plastic surgery, even though he thought she was fine the way she was, because then she'd get frantic, thinking he thought her crow's feet were really bad, and that he didn't love her anymore, he was going to find someone younger, and abandon her.

Head down, her hands holding each other, fingers feeling fingers. "I don't know why they have to call it crow's feet anyway. Why not just call it, I don't know, parakeet's feet. That even rhymes."

"I have a great surprise for you. You're really going to like this." And maybe this would distract her from worrying about her looks.

Rearing her head back. "You fixed the faucet? So I can finally sleep at night?"

"Even better." He went back to the front door of their apartment, opening it.

Her alarm. "I'm not going back, am I?" Quivering lip. She had only been out of the institute for five days since her most recent admission.

"No, no! This is a good thing!" Looking out into the corridor, whistling.

A short bald-headed man wearing a suit walked into their apartment. Beamed a big grin at Audrey.

"Noah? Who is he?"

"This is Bennie. He's a life coach. I know I can't be with you all the time, while I'm at work, and I know how sad that makes you, but now you'll have Bennie here to cheer you up!"

"Oh, I don't like this!"

"Mrs. Wright? Audrey? If I dare?" Palms patting the air in front of him. "I am here to put a smile on

161

your face. I am an expert at cheering people up, of putting a lilt in their step and an extra inch of booze in their glass. I will have you in stitches."

She tried to think of what to say. "Can you fix a leaky faucet?"

Pretend indignation. "Can I fix a leaky faucet? I can not only fix a leaky faucet, I can teach it to speak Spanish without a lisp, calculate Pi to the zillionth decimal, and bake a perfect French apple pie, the type with raisins inside and a white sugar icing on top. Take me to the culprit."

Audrey shyly led him into the kitchen. Pointed at the aluminum sink. "There."

The faucet was not dripping.

Bennie staggered back, clutching his chest. "It is loud, it is deafening, it's making me want to poop my pants. Let me get in there and roll up my sleeves, fair damsel, and I will send those drips back to the hellish fires from whence they came."

She watched as he got down on his back to slide through the opened cabinet doors under the sink, scramble back to his short height to twist the base of the faucet with a wrench.

Finished, he looked at her in triumph. "It is as tight as a South Dakota farm boy's ass, just before I tell him how blue his eyes are."

Audrey agreed they'd keep him.

Ⅱ

And her spirits did seem to pick up. Each evening over dinner, candlelight, it'd be Bennie this, Bennie that. Noah had seen her draw even further into herself after her dad died, and she stopped talking to her mom after a long telephone argument. Loudly grinding her teeth while he tried to fall asleep, worse than snores. She was the type of person who needed someone safe in addition to her husband to share confidences. And Bennie was all about confidences.

Once a week, he'd meet Bennie for lunch while Audrey was at the hairdresser's, to find out about her current mood.

"She's definitely connecting more with other people, especially checkout clerks, where there's a more-defined behavioral protocol. I can see her gaining confidence, to where she even made a joke with a salesgirl at Watkins Dresses. When someone is willing to risk making a joke, asking for a laugh, that's a real sign of improvement."

A month went by without Audrey having to return to the institute. She and Noah celebrated with lobsters. He pulled it all out of the cracked shell for her, hot and steaming, so her black plate was red and white meat, bowl of yellow butter. Two months. They became lovers again, some of Audrey's insecurities held at bay. And she was a great lover when the little green demons went away, sliding her stomach on top of his, eyes fierce.

Ⅱ

Bennie leaned across his side of the table. Waiters passing behind him. "They call this a salad? I could have performed the Heimlich maneuver on a rabbit, and what it threw up would be more appetizing than this."

Audrey giggled. "You always make me feel better. I'm so glad Noah found you for me."

"He's a grand guy, a true champ. The lovable mutt would do anything to put a smile on your face."

"Speaking of dogs, what pound did you find her in?"

Forks motionless, mid-air.

Bennie turned his face to the right. Tall, young guy sitting by himself at the next table. Port-red birthmark on his face. Staring at them, knowing how rude he was being. Getting off on it.

"How you doin', Stretch? Word of advice? Play nice with the lady or I'll zip up my fly and choke you to death."

Shrug meant to be insulting in its casualness. Picking at his fried kale. "Just saying. Can't teach an old dog new tricks."

"Not strictly true, sport. I was the one who taught your daddy how to angle his cock that crucial extra inch up your asshole while he's fucking you, so you'd be able to squirt just a little more jism on your mom's face. You think you know how to insult? Watching you try to be rude is like watching a rich person try to dance. Fuck off, string bean."

But he didn't. He started following Audrey and Bennie everywhere they went. While Audrey was inside the dressing room at a local shop, stepping out of her jeans to try on a skirt, she could hear, through the drawn-closed curtain, the two of them trading wisecracks out on the sales floor.

"What's wrong?" Noah sitting on Audrey's side of the bed, her eyes glistening, tears warmer than blood.

Little hands, curled inwards, waving in circles above her head. "There's this guy, this complete asshole, stupid birthmark on his face, he follows Bennie and me around wherever we go, and he—" voice strained—"keeps saying these horrible things about me!"

Noah's still face. "What guy? Where does he show up?"

"Everywhere! The ice cream shoppe, the art galleries on Sixth Street…"

"I'm going with you and Bennie tomorrow. You point him out to me. I'll take care of it."

High voice of a little girl. "You will? Promise?"

The three of them went to the cheese shop. Audrey sampled some Gorgonzola Dulce. No asshole.

Saw a performance of Beethoven's Waldstein. Bought, from a street vendor, burritos stuffed with Carne Adovada. Found just the right pink and green silk scarf at High Fineries. Sat through a demonstration of how Turkish taffy is made. No asshole.

Her phone rang. Got it out of her purse. Put it to her ear. Threw it away from her, like it was crawling on her head. "It's him! He just said my father never loved me!"

Noah bent down to the sidewalk, snatched up the phone. But the line was dead. Handed it back to her.

They didn't get five feet away before it rang again.

"Don't answer it."

They kept walking. The phone kept ringing. Audrey started crying.

Noah took the phone out of her purse. "Who is this?"

But the line was dead.

Back in her purse, it started ringing.

They were passing a wire wastebasket. "Let's throw it out. I'll buy you a new phone."

"But it has all my numbers on it!"

Bennie stepped up. "What a loser! A little momma's boy! He probably has one leg shorter than the other so he walks down the street at a tilt. If he was a house, he'd be a hovel. If he was an animal, he'd be roadkill. When he had a son the nurse brought him the newborn, threw it against the wall and said, April Fool! He was already dead."

165

But none of that helped.

A night later, waking up, her side of the bed empty, he followed the sound of her anguished voice to their bathroom. She was collapsed on the tile floor in front of their toilet, phone to her ear, eyes blinking, his poor wife babbling, trying to get the upper hand on the insults squawking from the phone, and failing, failing, time and again.

Ⅱ

The admissions nurse, Susie, gave Audrey a gentle smile. "You keep coming back!"

Audrey's sad, frightened face, trying to manage a smile. "I'm like a good penny."

Most of the staff knew her, of course. And Noah.

Once she was processed, and shown which room she'd get this time, the two of them walked hand in hand into the high-ceilinged noise of the common area. A lot of old faces. A lot of new faces.

"Are you just going to abandon me this time? Give up hope?"

He didn't want to cry, because she could so easily misunderstand his tears. "I'll never give up hope. Ever." Gave her frail shoulder a strong squeeze. "You're my wife. I'll visit you, just like before. And eventually, when you're ready, we'll start all over again. Like we always do."

He helped her into a chair by the window. She was having more and more difficulty walking. Stroked the back of her white hair. Looked down at her as she stared past the window. "I'll be back tomorrow to see how you're doing, okay?"

But she had already forgotten him. Lost in her own worries, small right hand up by her chin, two rows of teeth clicking against each other, eyes flicking left, right, fearfully.

♊

Routine can help people.

This is the time you're woken up. Made to dress.

This is the time you eat breakfast.

The time you take your morning pills, so it's not on an empty stomach.

The time you're led to the common area.

The time you eat lunch.

The time you take your afternoon pills, so it's not on an empty stomach.

The time you're returned to the common area.

The time you eat dinner.

The time you take your evening pills, so it's not on an empty stomach.

The time you're returned to the common area.

The time you're led back to your room.

The time you're woken up. Made to dress.

The common area was always so noisy. Rantings, TV sounds, mumblings. But she never found it that depressing. She'd inch her way over to her favorite chair, by the windows, hands behind her, tongue between her lips, carefully maneuvering herself down into the seat. Stare out the window.

And out there, somewhere, are the two of them. This little girl who's all grown up but confused, just can't get away, no matter where she sits in the restaurant, from the sunlight in her eyes, and this little boy she saw in a TV interview in the common room a long, long time ago, getting weaker and weaker. And they are out there, somewhere. Her coming home from her latest stay at the latest institution, Noah has a banner hanging across their living room ceiling, Welcome Back, they cook a great meal together, but then turn off the burners and go in back, to the bedroom, to make love, he's bought

167

a cat for her, it's so loving, it jumps up on her lap, looking up at her, the jewel eyes, the purring, Noah comes in with a wrench in his hand, There's something wrong with the air-conditioning, it's not working, but don't worry, I'll call the repair shop in the morning, they finish their meal, and the noise outside her closed eyes is increasing, screams, pleas, channels being changed, arguments, sobbing, shouted commands, so she has to picture everything in even greater detail, that's the only way it works, not the steak but the pat of butter melting atop the steak, magnified until it fills her mind, until she can see, fully see, how that molten pat is paler in its center, see the yellow rivulets slide down, mixing on the white plate with the pink juice exuded from the brown steak. But when she cuts her first ruby slice, and lifts its red and golden drippings to her happy lips, chewing, the butter is not good, it's a bit rancid, actually quite rancid. Very much rancid. She has to lower her head, as if for execution, open her mouth, and let that otherwise wonderful slice of steak fall out from between her teeth, onto the beautiful white plate.

Ⅱ

It helps when nurses are pretty.

Samantha hovers her dark eyes above Noah's face. The beep of monitoring equipment.

"I'm going to ask you to count backwards from one hundred, okay? In your mind."

Looking up at her, looking up at the sun, he gives a wobbly smile.

His hands holding each other, fingers feeling fingers.

"Now, I know a big boy like you isn't scared, right?"

"Nope!" Don't know how brave that came out, but he desperately wants to impress her, because what fourteen year old boy wouldn't want to impress a pretty nurse?

"That's my hero! And when you wake up, you're going to have all new bone marrow. Healthy bone marrow! So…one hundred…"

One hundred.

He thought about his mom. He knew his cancer drove her and his dad to get a divorce, but he was hopeful that once he was finally cured, they'd get back together again. He even knew how he'd do it. His birthday was coming up. Take them both out to dinner, with the money he had saved, and near the end of the meal, all three of them happy, he'd be the voice of reason, saying to both of them, Mom, Dad, you know you love each other. Let's be a family again.

Ninety-nine.

Early in this process, even though he was just a little kid, he decided he was never going to show his fear. Inside, in his head, he was terrified, and he saw so many boys and girls at the hospital whose eyes glistened, whose red faces crumpled when it was their turn to be called in, but he decided he would be different. He'd show his mom and dad, but later just his dad, that they had a brave boy. That they had a boy who was willing to be wheeled into a white room where no child should ever have to go, and have needles pushed into his thin arms, and have big machines mounted to the white ceiling swung over his tense body, so his insides could be burned.

Ninety-eight.

He had long ago forgotten what normal was. When he wasn't being hurt by all these smiling adults in their white clothes. When did it end? When he was on his knees, planting those snapdragons? That boy died that day. This was a new boy. A stronger, less happy boy.

Ninety-seven.

And now he could sense the black, wavy fingers of the intravenous anesthesia entering his mind from both sides. Before it was too late, before he slipped under, he went to his favorite fantasy. Him an adult, tall, broad-shouldered, and strong. He's cured. Driving down the road he and his parents used to take, to bring their dog to the vet for shots. And a woman, a beautiful, dark-haired woman crashes into his car. Like it was a movie.

Ninety-six.

And then it came, as it always did. The darkness.

Welcome back, Noah.

The Wrong House

Tracy Fahey

I wake up in the morning and I'm in the wrong house. I get out of the wrong bed and put on the wrong clothes. Downstairs the wrong wife is making breakfast for the wrong child. I stand in the striped shadow of the bannisters as I watch them; a world apart, in a bright bubble of cornflakes and sunshine and chatter. I don't say anything. Instead I pick up the wrong briefcase and walk out the wrong door. And suddenly I'm in a world of rightness. I look around me at the familiar objects, counting them off, the words matching the images, reassuring me. Sky. Hedges. Cars. Bus. *Good*. My feet press firmly into a crunchy, sifting layer of gravel. I take in a deep breath. *I've been working too hard*, I think, half-nodding as I do so. I look around, breathing in the stale fumes of the traffic, the smell punchy and real in my nostrils. *Funny the tricks your mind plays on you.*

And then my smug inner monologue dies. I've glanced behind me. And there it is. The Wrong House. It has a varnished wooden gate, not a painted one. There's a pink bicycle in the yard but there should be a green one. The house itself has too many windows. The paintwork on the exterior is almost the right colour, but not. The prints of my feet in the loose gravel have vanished. The house stands there, solid and undistinguished in the pearly morning light; standing comfortably, shoulder to shoulder, camouflaged with its innocent neighbours. As I stand and look at it a wave of sickness burns at the back of my throat.

It's *wrong*. It's all wrong. It's so wrong it hurts my stomach.

171

"You OK, Tom?" It's one of my elderly neighbours. Her puckered eyes are soft with concern. I suddenly see myself as she sees me, sweating, staring, hands gripping my briefcase with white-streaked knuckles. For a moment I'm tempted to tell her the truth. But only for a moment.

I stand up straight and shake my head. "I'm alright," I say shortly. And I mean it. I'm right. Alright. It's the house that's wrong.

The Wrong House. The Wrong House. It thumps through my head like a refrain as I wait for the bus.

Ⅱ

But where is the Right House? Sitting on the bus, I close my eyes and visualise it, see myself opening the right gate, walking confidently into the right house, where the right wife is cooking dinner and laughing at my strange fancy. I see her pick up the right daughter…

My eyes fly open. *Where is my daughter?* The bus looks suddenly alien; I see the passengers sitting like bundles of clothing. Their mouths move but I don't hear anything. Underneath my seat, the vibrations of the bus hum through me, deep and insistent. If the wrong daughter is at home with the wrong wife, where are they? My family. The Right Family. I think about getting off the bus and catching one back, just to see if everything has righted itself, but a glance at my watch tells me I'm late.

When I arrive at the office block the doorman looks at me strangely. "I don't have your pass here," he says, checking through the book. "It says here you're on leave."

"I…I…" I'm stammering, confused. Am I on leave? Should I go home? It all seems wrong, deeply wrong. I walk towards the bus stop, then pause. Am I

172

ready to see the wrong family again? I look down at my hands. They're trembling. So I sit down at a pavement café across the road and order the first of many coffees.

When evening falls, I see them troop out, my co-workers. I want to talk to them but something holds me back. Inside the building is still illuminated against the navy-dim sky. I can see the cleaners are humming around the building when I get up to leave.

By the time I get home, the light has faded to black. I can't see The Wrong House as I approach it, just its murky outline. It looks comfortingly familiar. If I ignore the fact the door handle is different, I can almost believe everything is fine. The house itself is silent. Everyone is in bed. I don't put a light on. I simply stand, motionless in the darkness, inside the front door and feel the deep breathing upstairs, long, low waves of it, spreading across the house. It's enough to relax me. That is, until I get upstairs and the wrong wife is sleeping on the wrong side of the wrong bed.

I back away and walk carefully downstairs, feeling my way to the sofa, where I lie, tense and wakeful. The coffees of the day return to haunt me; I can almost see the brown liquid pumping erratically around my body. Finally, I doze off into an uneasy sleep.

II

"Silly Daddy." I open my eyes to see the wrong toddler smiling at me, her head tilted to one side. She is so cute that for a moment I just smile back, before remembering, and sitting up with a jerk. Instantly my heart sinks. I'm still in the Wrong House. The table is on the wrong side of the room. There is an unknown cereal box on the table. My wife's hair is blonde, not

173

this orangey-amber. She smiles at me, but her eyes are worried, circled with black.

"Leave Daddy alone," she says gently to the little girl. "Daddy's tired." My headache throbs hard as a heartbeat. She bends over me, her amber hair swishing over her shoulders. I close my eyes and feel her soft hand on my forehead. For a second her cool hand feels so good, I almost try and persuade myself its real. That it's right.

"Where are they?" I blurt out, before I can stop myself.

"Who?" Her eyes are puzzled now. She touches my forehead again. *The Right Family*, I think, in an agony of confusion.

"Your forehead's hot," she says, her voice sharp with worry. I open my eyes, and flinch at the bright sunlight that floods the room.

"Remember what day it is. Look at the calendar," she says. I try to, but the colourful marker scribbles hurt my eyes. I see my own name, 'Tom' written and circled around today's date. (The calendar, of course, is wrong, no longer a succession of images of Gaudi's Barcelona, but a montage of husky puppies.) I wave a hand at the wrong wife, tell her I'm late and escape before I have to look at the wrongness anymore.

Where are you?

It's not until I'm at the bus-stop that I feel my headache start to subside.

II

I sit in vigil again, careful to sit out of the eye line of the doorman. This time when work finishes, I stand up. I'm looking for someone. Graham. He works at the desk beside mine. I don't like Graham, but at least he is the right Graham, red-faced, a slight roll of neck-flab, portly physique straining out of his navy-blue suit.

I fall into step beside him. "Want to go for a beer?"

"Tom! How have you been." His rotund face is full of queries.

"Oh you know,' I say evasively. 'Are you coming for a drink?"

He says yes. Of course he does. I know he will. It's his favourite thing to do, a pint after work. I don't want to be on my own tonight. Not in The Wrong House.

When we sit at the bar, the conviction deepens. I just don't want to go home. I keep offering to refill his drink, anxious for him to stay. We're on our fourth pint when I bring it up.

"Did you ever feel…," I hesitate, searching for the right term. "Discombobulated?" His face is blank. I try again. "Out of time? Displaced? In the wrong universe?"

"Only every morning in work!" He laughs fatly at his own joke, double-chin wobbling.

I ignore him and keep going. "Say you woke up and felt you were in the wrong place?"

Now he's listening. "Like waking up in someone else's place after a party?"

"Kind of." I pause, and then elaborate. "More like waking up somewhere you actually know really well but it looks strange. Unfamiliar." I stop and take a long swallow of beer. "Because that's how I feel every morning."

He's stopped laughing. "When did this start?"

"A few days ago. I thought it would pass, but it didn't." The relief of telling someone, even prosaic old Graham from work, is giddying. "Everything just looks…wrong. The furniture, the rooms, even the outside of the house."

"Mate," says Graham. "The doc said something like this might happen. Remember?" Somewhere deep inside of me I feel a surge of fear. The empty pint glass slips through my slippery fingers. The crash is oddly cathartic. I look down at the glittering sprinkle of glass splinters.

"No," I say. "I don't. Don't remember."

"The accident, mate." Graham is looking at me carefully. "Your accident. Bump on the head, he said. Sometimes causes a bit of confusion, he said."

I stand up to go, swaying slightly, a combination of beer and a sudden wash of terror. My shirt is clinging damply to my back. "Yes," I say, my lips moving over each other with some difficulty. "Yes, of course."

I don't remember the bus journey. Not the bus, not the passengers, not the driver, not the journey. I feel like I've just blinked—just one blink—and I'm home. Or at The Wrong House, anyhow. It's not as late as I thought; the sky has just purpled into dusk. I move my hand to knock on the unfamiliar door, then shake my head and take out my keys. The wrong wife is waiting for me inside. No sign of our daughter. She doesn't hesitate, but launches straight in.

"Where have you been?"

"Work," I say, then add truthfully, "and the pub. With Graham."

"That loser! You don't even like him! And why didn't you call me? I've been so worried." I hear her voice catch, snag on a sob, then recover. "I even rang the hospital."

"The hospital?"

"You were meant to ring me after your check-up. Don't you remember?" Her voice cracks in frustration. With a sudden pang I remember seeing my name written on the calendar. I flick a glance at

176

it. Yes, there it is. Circled in the wrong marker, on the wrong calendar.

"As if it's not bad enough, dealing with your moodiness and silence! Since the accident you've been impossible to live with. Like today—you can't even be bothered to let me know how your check-up went. When I've been going out of my mind here!" She covers her face, and her body convulses with deep, grating sobs. I move to hold her out of instinct, although my mind is crying out *amber hair, wrong dress*, but she puts out a hand to ward me off.

"Don't..." she says. I stand there, helplessly, memories flickering just out of reach. *An accident?* I have some vague memories of dazzling fluorescent lights overhead, a sensation of movement, a flash of pain... and then I shake my head and it's gone.

She raises a wet face to me. "I'm tired," she says limply. "So tired. I can't deal with the coldness anymore. The silence. You've completely changed. I love you, but I can't stay here. Neither can she. She's too small"—her voice breaks, then steadies itself—"She's too small to understand. So we're going."

For the first time I realise that there is a neat pile of suitcases at the door. Unfamiliar ones, naturally, but there's no mistaking their meaning. Our wrong daughter appears at the top of the stairs. *Where are you?* I think, and my face is wet with tears for my missing daughter.

But when they stand at the doorstep, I feel a pang of loss. They may be the wrong family, but they're the only one I have.

"I'm sorry," I say uselessly.

"Too little," she says, grabbing the handles of the cases. "And way too late."

Just before the door shuts, she turns and half-smiles, but tears are running down her face. *Where are you?* I wonder. And then she's gone, and I'm left behind. On my own. In The Wrong House.

♊

I don't sleep so well that night. I lie there and think— *what's happened to me?* At about four o'clock I give up, get up, and yank open drawers, looking for journals, notepads, correspondence, anything at all that might offer a clue. At seven o'clock I admit defeat, shower and dress. By a quarter to eight I'm standing at the bus stop in front of The Wrong House, perfectly attired and freshly shaved. On the surface, at least, I'm ready for work. In fact, I'm about to get on the bus, when I hesitate. Surely there's someone in the hospital who can tell me what's going on?

I'm in the admissions area, standing patiently by the reception desk when my phone vibrates in my pocket. It's Graham.

"Tom. I've been thinking about yesterday. Are you OK? We never talked about it. You know…" His voice trails off.

"No," I say. "We didn't."

"It's just, I've been thinking, do you want to talk?"

"Not right now, I say. I'm in hospital." And I'm not quite sure why but after I press 'End Call' I drop my phone in the waste bin.

I go back to the desk and explain who I am and about missing my appointment yesterday. Of course I don't have any letter on me, or any memory of making an appointment, but the efficient girl at the desk has tracked me down.

"Your name is Tom Albright? Address 39 Meadowbrook, Mill Estates? Ah. Head Trauma. You had an appointment with consultant Mr. Brown?" It sounds right, so I nod. She smiles, satisfied. "Now we

178

don't have a record of any cancellation, so I'm afraid we haven't rescheduled." Her brows knot as she jabs at the keyboard. "Take a seat for a while, and I'll see if I can do anything for you."

The hours tick by. All around me is drama and confusion and an endless medley of voices and motion. I sit patiently, waiting. I don't mind it. At least I'm not in the house. From my seat I can hear my phone buzz repeatedly in the wastepaper bin, until it finally stops. The battery must have died. Now I'm non-contactable. I inhale deeply, stretch out, and read the 'Signs of a Stroke' poster yet again.

"Tom! Tom, isn't it?" It's a small, dark doctor in a rumpled while coat. He looks familiar. He's smiling and shaking my hand. "So good to see you!"

"Good to see you too," I say weakly. "I missed my appointment yesterday, so I'm just…" I trail off, suddenly unsure as to why exactly I'm here. He looks at me closely.

"It's just that I'm seeing strange things. In my home." The doctor (his lapel says Dr. Khalid) checks his watch, and then raises his eyebrows at me.

"I have a few minutes. Do you want to talk?" I nod and follow him down a green, antiseptic corridor to a small office. He moves a pile of files from the chair to the floor, then stands, thinking, before scuffling around his desk for a notebook.

"Here we are," he says happily, brandishing a blue notepad. His face is tired, but his manner is so cheerful, I can't help warming to him. "I took these notes when you were admitted a year ago. They were on my desk in case the good Mr. Brown needed them yesterday." He sits down and takes a pen from his pocket. "So, please start."

"Well," I begin. I'm taken aback at how promptly he's agreed to see me—I'm under-rehearsed and unsure where exactly to start. "It's just stuff that's been happening over the last week. Maybe longer. I don't know if it's my memory or if it's my brain playing tricks on me. Or if it's them, and they've really changed." I see I'm not making sense, so I plunge on. "You know, maybe it is my memory. I don't really remember you, for example. But I remember everything in work. Everyone."

"OK, OK." He is busily writing it down. "So where are you experiencing these strange memories."

"At home." I say flatly. "I can't help but think I'm in the wrong house. Everything looks off to me— wrong colours, wrong rooms, wrong things…" I pause and shake my head to try and clear it. "Even my wife, my daughter…"

He looks up. "What about your wife and daughter?"

"They're different. They look differently to how I remember them. They act differently. They're *wrong*."

He's stopped writing now and is starting at me with a queer urgency in his eyes. I ask him the question that's been haunting me.

"Doctor—do I have amnesia?"

"Some symptoms of it," he says carefully. "The brain is a very delicate mechanism, and head trauma has many unexpected effects. Some things you remember, some things you don't. But I'm more concerned with what you say about your family."

"They've left me." I say quietly. It's the first time I've said it out loud. It hurts, but in a weirdly disconnected way.

He sighs and lays down his pen. "Yes. Yes they have."

I hear his words, but can't understand them. There's a dipping, vertiginous feeling, as if the floor beneath me is slowly melting.

Dimly, I become aware that the doctor is still speaking.

"Tom, your mind has constructed scenarios. Do you understand?" His eyes are tired, the corners creased in a network of lines. "We should have had more regular check-ups here," he says, half to himself. Then he sits up and speaks to me, slowly and clearly. "Tom. You've created this fantasy for yourself to help you through this difficult period. Now the scenario is starting to crumble and your brain is grappling with itself to understand."

I've been prepared for this. "So I'm going mad," I say simply.

The doctor stares at me. "No," he says finally. "I said this is a fantasy you've constructed. Your family home. Your family. I know some part of you understands this."

I look at him, frightened. *A fantasy?* My stomach clenches and I'm suddenly in a sick, trembling vortex of unreality. My certainty falls away. I'm helpless and lost. And then they start coming. The flashes of memory. The nauseating crump of being shunted hard in the back, the helpless, endless skid, the splintering crash. And then there's blood and shouting, and shining lights and men lifting me. And then a silence so huge I get swallowed up in it. My mouth is moving and screaming but there's no sound. There's nothing at all. There's no one there.

And then I understand. I understand all right. I've built it all myself. My wife, my daughter, my home. I've built it. I've built it all.

I am the architect of The Wrong House.

Little Heart

Georgina Bruce

This woman liked to break things. She'd always liked breaking things, ever since she was a child. Breaking, unmaking, unfolding, undoing, prising off, detaching, violently abstracting, dropping, smashing, crushing, agitating, neglecting, disconnecting. Whatever it took. She liked to break things with precision. She liked the moment of breakage, the moment when the broken thing came into existence and the thing it was before ceased to exist. She said, "Only when something breaks can you finally understand its true function and character. It's a process of physical deduction. It's graphic." She explained how she would pull the transistors out of radios, cut off her dolls' hands with scissors, slice worms in half with a penknife. "But it's unpredictable. Like splitting the atom. Such a tiny thing. What a big surprise inside!" She would say this sort of thing in classes and her students would take note. They hung off her words. She would see them in the bargain shop on Saturday afternoons, buying cheap crockery for smashing. "Break plates," she told them. "Break everything in the house."

Plates were one thing. But what this woman— let's call her Anna—what Anna really wanted to break were mirrors. And not just mirrors. She wanted to break windows. She wanted to break a house in half. Tear it apart in her hands. Just like tearing dough, except it would be floorboards and shingles and furniture stretching and breaking, and people falling out. She wanted to break noses. She wanted to break things made of glass and things made of bone. She had a passion for it.

Passion ran in her family.

Her mother had been passionate. She'd been an actress, briefly, and she'd starred in a film that had been popular for a while the year Anna turned seven. It was a black and white film, because in those days, they were all black and white. Her mother won an award for acting in it, a silver twist of metal on a wooden plinth—it was given pride of place in their sitting room, placed high up on a shelf. Anna was forbidden from touching it, of course. She'd been taken to see the film in a picture house, but her father had removed her when she became *disturbed and agitated* (as the doctor said later, pulling on his nose in an unpleasant manner.) The film's themes and images were certainly too adult for a small child to appreciate, even one as precocious as Anna. Perhaps her parents hadn't realised how inappropriate it was to take her to the picture house that night. Anna was over-sensitive, liable to make a drama over the littlest thing.

Anna remembered that evening as a fulcrum upon which the world balanced. From that point it tipped and swung between two dimensions. There was the real world that she had relied upon. And then there was a horrible new dimension. It was the sight of her mother on screen that had precipitated the breakdown. The woman looked like her mother—her exact, identical twin. But Anna saw she was wrong. It was not her mother. She saw that her mother had disappeared, been forced out by someone else— someone who inhabited her completely, and drove her to terrible extremes. There was one scene in particular—a celebrated scene—that had terrified Anna beyond her ability to endure, beyond the possibilities of her father's presence to console. In fact, it was then Anna realised she was alone in the world.

Early on in the film, the wrong mother is seen standing alone in a dining room. She is newly married. She wears a long black nightdress, sheer lace and silk trailing about her bare feet. Her lips and nails are painted red, but on film they look black. There is the sound of breaking glass. The camera pulls back to take her in. She's dropping wine glasses onto the stone floor. A piece of glass skims the top of her foot and a black wet seam opens. A ball of blood runs down between her toes. She doesn't react. She keeps dropping glasses onto the floor until there are shards and splinters and chunks of broken glass glinting all around her. Her feet are cut and bloodied. The camera shows us her hands, crossed with scars and wet with blood. But it's her face that arrests the viewer: her eyes. Her pupils are dark liquid haloed by ice. And the expression in them—she is lost inside herself, her madness.

When Anna saw this she knew she'd been wrong about everything. No one could now be trusted. Her mother could not even be trusted to remain housed in her own body! Anna guessed it was then, at the height of her distress in the picture house, that her long, confusing estrangement from her mother had begun. It had budded out from that moment, finally fruiting when Anna left home at seventeen, and then hardening as the years went by and drew the two women further and further apart. When Anna's mother died, Anna realised that she remembered the facsimile, the creepy ersatz mother, more vividly and powerfully than the real thing.

Anna thought she was nothing like her mother. On the other hand, she wasn't completely sure. She sometimes wondered if she was the rightful inhabitant of her body or whether another person was simply putting her on and off like a coat. It seemed to her that it was impossible to know. She could be a

184

character in a film, like her mother had been. Celluloid and ink instead of flesh and blood. Of course, Anna would prefer a beautiful film, like the one with all the thin, good-looking sad people having a party, while a massive asteroid hurtles towards the earth. If she died that way, would she know? Would there be time, in the moment of death, to see exactly what had made her tick with life? She hoped it would be a big surprise. She hoped when death came, she would be able to leave the machine of her body and enter the soft machine of the sky. She worried she would grieve for her body, not that it was a remarkable or beautiful body. If anything, she loathed it for its ugliness. But there was no knowing if you could do anything worthwhile without a body: it seemed like you probably needed one. Then again, what if she were just like her mother: a collection of images layered over one another, one over another to create the illusion of moving and talking. Then her ugly body might last forever. Like her mother's body was still, always, walking around an old haunted house, wearing strange old-fashioned clothes and speaking in an odd, pretty voice.

Anna had recently seen her mother's dead body in a casket, her face waxy and coated in make-up. She had once again put on a different body, only this one looked nothing like her. It seemed to have nothing to do with her, at all.

II

Anna's mother had been found half-naked on the kitchen floor, surrounded by broken glass. The death certificate said natural causes. The doctor told Anna she'd had a stroke, a massive one. She said it would have killed her instantly.

Her funeral attracted quite a crowd—mostly

extended family, some of whom had flown in from Israel and claimed to remember meeting Anna as a young girl. They spoke to her in Hebrew and Anna shook her head. "But you used to be absolutely fluent!" They prompted her with words and sayings, trying to coax the little girl out of her. It was impossible—they remembered a different child altogether. Anna was quite sure that none of these people had ever sung to her, dandled her on their laps, or listened enraptured to her childish recitations of poems and songs in their language. Those things had never happened. (However, when pressed, Anna admitted she remembered nothing much of her childhood before the trauma of the picture house. Everything that came before then had been erased from her mind.) She guessed her family were disappointed to see she had not lived up to her mother's beauty.

No one mentioned Anna's father. No one ever spoke of him, not since the day he'd left. Anna wondered if he'd be at the funeral, but she wouldn't have recognised him even if he had been. She couldn't remember what he looked like. Only his handsome, serious eyes, and the gloss of his hair.

The family were kind and made a fuss over Anna, but she was embarrassed by their sympathy. She didn't want it. They thought she must be broken-hearted, but what she had felt most in the few days after her mother's death was a strange heady kind of freedom. The doctor called it shock. She felt herself expanding, growing taller. She walked faster, feeling that the range of her legs and arms had increased, that there was energy powering through her. She grew in strength and stature. She decided her mother's death was the best thing that had ever happened to her, and rather than sympathy, she wanted a celebration.

Of course, someone spoke of the film. Although it

186

had been mostly forgotten by the rest of the world, the family still thought it wonderful that one of theirs had been famous and celebrated. Anna avoided those conversations, but was prompted to recall she still had a copy of the film on videotape. She couldn't think why she'd kept it all these years. She'd kept it even after the video player became obsolete, and she'd thrown all her other tapes away. But she'd never even taken it from the back of the shelf where it was hidden. She wasn't afraid to watch it—it was just irrelevant, of no interest. It couldn't hurt her, break her, psychically dislocate her, force her out of her body and into her previous incarnation... a child screaming in the cinema, wetting her pants, her father pinning her arms behind her back. Of course not. The past was over and there was nothing to be frightened of. And Anna had made her peace, more or less, with her own self now. Despite all her failures, she'd survived nearly sixty years of life. She made art, she was good at it, and validated for it, and paid. Now her mother was finally gone, leaving behind a space for Anna to stretch out into. Why should she put herself through the experience of watching the film? She decided she never would. She would find it and throw it away. Better still, she would smash the casing and unspool the tape and set it on fire.

But that is not what happened.

II

The wrong mother breaks a mirror and her face is fractured into a thousand pieces. The screen is full of pieces, a cacophony of faces. ("Perhaps the film was too grown up for you," Anna's father said. "You embarrassed your mother. You embarrassed me. Everyone was looking at you." Anna associated this memory with the taste of raspberries, and

187

remembered her father crushing up tablets into red syrup, using the back of a spoon. For a while afterwards, a long time, she felt she was breathing underwater; everyone's voices streamed in distorted bubbles towards a surface she could not break.)

The wrong mother wakes up in the middle of the night. She lights a candle. Her husband is nowhere to be seen. As she casts the candle around, it sheds light and definition on the faces in the wallpaper, and the faces in the crumpled sheets, and the faces in the grain of the wood on the door. She walks, barefoot as always, through the house, holding her candle bravely in front of her. She is looking for him. She whispers his name. Down the staircase and then across the great hall and into the kitchen, where a fire still glows in the range. But where is he? She opens the door to the cellar. Darkness. The candle sputters but the light holds, enough for the wrong mother to pick her way down the stairs. Halfway down she almost slips. She clutches at the banister. It's velvety with moss. There's water lapping at her feet. Then her candle is blown out.

When the light next comes, she is walking through water up to her waist, wading out onto a small sandy beach, beyond which another house stands. It is identical to her own house, there are lights on in all the windows. She's wearing the black lace nightdress again, only now it is soaked through and clinging to her frozen skin. There is a sudden black flapping of wings and the screen is full of birds, pecking and hopping, their eyes glinting cruelly, until somehow they resolve themselves into the shape of a man.

II

Anna's father had been nothing like that man. Of this

Anna was quite certain—but she watched him closely all the same. Anna's father was handsome, and smelled like the inside of his briefcase. Paper and ink. He wore a heavy watch that had to be wound twice a day. He gave Anna books on her birthday and at Christmas. He called her 'little heart' and 'little thing' and said she was pretty when she knew she was not. When she told him she planned to become an artist, he didn't laugh. But after the incident in the picture house, he was different. He was a photograph fading, a memory of a father. He began to remind Anna of the man in the film, the feathered man with his cruel beak. It was silly, really. Just the way he looked at her sometimes.

Since Anna was under sedation, she didn't keep regular waking and sleeping hours. She moved through the days in a syrupy fugue, not quite knowing if it was time for breakfast or time to go to bed. When she woke up in the middle of the night, she thought it could just as easily be the middle of the day. Her perspective was distorted. She would spend long hours sitting in front of a mirror, in a low light, watching as her face became a stranger's face. She watched her father's face just as intently, every time she had a chance. She sometimes thought she saw her father's eye glint glossy-black, and the dull sheen of his beak, the tender attachments where smooth beak grew from soft tiny feathers. Even in the daytime, Anna's father grew darker, and bigger, or was it that Anna was growing smaller and lighter. (Like Alice, she was always too big or too small, or too far away or too dissolved into the air, or something.)

Anna woke up in the middle of the night. She was too weak and dizzy to remember her dream. But certain things came back to her: the sound of a door slamming in the top of her head, and the knowledge that *he* was in the house—and that he wanted her for

189

something—that he had broken her mother wide open and now it was Anna's turn. In the dream, she remembered seeing his face looming towards her, his beak about to pierce the flesh of her cheek. His wings were enormous; his feathers were dirty and smelled of trash.

After the dream, Anna was desperate to see her father right away. Just to prove to herself that he *was* her father, and not a terrible bird thing. She would sneak into her parents' room, quickly look upon his handsome sleeping face, and be relieved of the evil dream. But when she had tiptoed across the landing, she saw a light edging the heavy door, and heard what sounded like a whispered argument—they argued all the time in those days. Anna didn't want to see her parents while they were awake. She was afraid of their anger, knowing from experience it could be deflected onto her simply because she was there. But she was far more afraid of the thing her father had been in her dream. She had to see him. So she pushed open the door.

At first she didn't understand. Then she realised she wasn't awake after all, and the dream was still inside her, dreaming her out. There was a black cloak of feathers over the bed, lustrous and crawling with lice. Her mother was naked, on all fours facing the door. There was blood on her beautiful face and breasts and arms. Anna's father was behind her mother, rocking back and forth from his hips. It wasn't her father. It was the dream of her father as a bird, as the man-bird from the film. He looked at Anna and his cruel face twisted into a smile. He licked his lips. He pushed her mother's head down into the feathers and rocked faster as he watched Anna watching him. She felt paralysed, unable to breathe, impossible to even close her eyes. She hated his gleeful expression, the noises he was making, the way his claws dug into the back of her mother's head... Anna concentrated on moving just one part of herself, her little finger... if she could do it, she'd wake up. But it wasn't possible. Later, she remembered this moment not as a dream, but as though it were a film stopped in the middle of a scene, the actor immobilised, her face embalmed in its expression of horror—yet her father and mother were the real show, images moving fast enough to blur skin and feathers, blood and tears. Anna was paused in her place. Then suddenly, without warning, the film unstuck. She took a deep breath, clenched her fists, turned, ran.

It was a dream. Her child's imagination running riot, the strong sedatives enveloping her in their heavy weirdness. Even the next afternoon, when she pulled a soft black feather from her thigh, leaving a little bloody hole, Anna could see that this was only because she had mixed up dreams with films and fantasy with reality. She had invented everything, wicked little fantasist that she was. She always believed it was this that had driven her father away. Her ugliness, her madness that night—he had somehow known how disgusting she was. And that is why, the next morning, he was gone.

II

In the days after the funeral, Anna's new energy wore thin. She talked too much in class, was impatient, accused her students of being intellectually weak, lacking in purpose. She mocked their work, sent them away with her laughter ringing in their ears. Her head of department said she was too harsh, there had been complaints. Anna countered with passion. She just wanted them to find fractures in their protective middle-class veneer. "Find where it hurts and then dig away there with the sharpest thing you can find," she told them. But her students had trouble recognising their own fault lines. They defaulted to physical violence, to accidents. They were always coming to class with bruises and cuts and their arms in slings. One time, she was speaking with a student she hadn't seen for a while. "I had a heart attack," he told her. She wanted to ask him, "And did it work? Did it open you up?" Instead she said, "Show me the scar." He lifted his t-shirt and she let her eyes trace the sore red weal bisecting his chest. She wanted to slide a craft knife along its length and lever him open again.

The head of department told Anna to take some time off. A family bereavement is a serious matter, she said. Perhaps Anna should talk to someone. By *someone* she meant, of course, a therapist of some kind. "You don't seem yourself," she said. Anna said she was fine. Who was she, if not herself? But she didn't want to hear the answer to this question. She thought she already knew the answer. Not that she could prove it, but it seemed to her she was less real every day. She thought her skin had changed, that her eyes had grown darker; at times she noticed her movements were almost imperceptibly jerky, as though she were an image, stuttering on screen. A series of images layered one over the other, one after another to create the illusion of her body.

Just like her mother.

To prove she was really nothing like her mother, Anna knew she would have to watch the film. And once she had taken the tape down from the shelf, Anna realised she had no choice. The tape had a certain weight, an animus that Anna responded to. She was an artist, after all. Maybe it wouldn't be such a frightening thing, to watch this film again, now, as an adult. She'd no doubt laugh at the stupid special

192

effects and wobbly scenery and terrible acting. Perhaps she wouldn't even recognise what had frightened her back then—it was only the irrationality of a child who didn't understand what it means to play act at being someone else. A sick child who couldn't understand the difference between a film, a dream, and the real world.

It was all in the past and there was nothing to be frightened of. In fact, Anna suspected that once enough time has elapsed, the past is erased and collapsed out of existence. Time breaks everything. Time is really just another word for breakage: every hour self destructs, every second is irretrievably snapped and broken with the ticking of a watch.

Ⅱ

Anna had to go into the cellar to find the video player, which was bigger and heavier than she remembered. It took a while to make it work—the drawer mechanism was jammed and she had to unscrew the front of it and put it back together. When she put the tape into the player, she found it had not been rewound, and it began to play from the middle of the film, the part after the wrong mother washes up on the beach, and follows the wrong man to the wrong house. Anna felt quite calm looking at the wrong mother's face. It was the man who frightened Anna now.

The wrong mother has to be punished for leaving her room. There are intimate sacrifices to be made: her tongue, her hair, her eyes. But for now, they are dancing. He is an excellent dancer. He turns her around the floor until she's dizzy, clinging on to his shoulders, falling against him. The film is not explicit. But somehow the scene is erotic. The way he lifts her hair from her neck. She bites her lip. He

193

grips her waist. She looks away. Anna felt afraid for the wrong mother. Something bad would happen. Something bad was happening. She didn't want to watch, but she forced herself to see, through the cracks in her fingers, what happened next.

Ⅱ

But no one sees what happens to the wrong mother that night. To her eyes and her tongue and her hair. It all takes place under the cover of his darkness. The humid cloak of his wings, the trap of his beak, all of his sharp dark vicious pecking—there is nothing to see. It is all left to the imagination.

Then later, she sits by her window in the dim, shadowy bedroom. By candlelight, her expression registers pain. She lifts her nightdress to the tops of her thighs. There is a curled black feather on her leg, the shaft piercing the skin. She plucks it out, and a bead of blood plummets down her thigh, dropping onto the floor beneath the chair.

Anna's hands flew to her mouth. She remembered this exact thing happening to *her*—the tiny soft black feather, the welling of her blood—it seemed so real, this memory, it was shocking to see it played out on screen, to realise it wasn't a memory at all, but something that had happened to someone else. Not even that—to realise it had never happened at all, not in reality. Anna had always known that memories couldn't be trusted, but she was shocked all the same. She could still feel the pinch of pain as she plucked the feather from her thigh, she could vividly remember seeing the blood well out of the tiny hole in her skin. But that was a fiction. All the past is a fiction. The past—what she thought of as her childhood—it was only a film she'd watched, a stupid fairytale that gave her nightmares. It was the dream and the film all tangled together in the soft knots of her brain.

♊

The wrong mother sits before a mirror. She cuts off her hair with a pair of silver scissors. Her hair is black and glossy and falls away from her in silken ropes. She cuts her hair short, leaving just an uneven shock to halo her head. With her hair gone, she is even more beautiful than before. You see the hollows of her cheeks, the darkness under her eyes. When she looks into the mirror again, she sees him standing behind her, and gasps. In her only true act of resistance in the film, she wrenches the mirror away from its stand and throws it across the room to where he should be standing, but suddenly no longer is. The mirror smashes, and a shard of it curves through the air, pierces her skin, slides through her ribcage and stabs her in the heart.

How utterly depressing, Anna thought—the first time she manages to stand up for herself, it kills her. And the man-bird is completely free, untouched by her death. Even when the police come for her body, there is no mention of a man, no mention of a husband at all. It makes you wonder if there was ever such a person, or whether the whole thing was just in her head. This is infuriating, too. Now the viewer doubts her sanity, her recollection of events, her victimhood. Perhaps she was only ever abusing herself, like a Victorian girl putting needles inside her urethra, having hysterics and crying rape.

Anna was infuriated by the ending of the film. It's so stupid, so pointless. She recalled her parents arguing about it—her father saying that the woman had lost her mind, that she was a fantasist and weak-minded and insane. Her mother crying with

195

frustration, insisting the real story is precisely that no one believes her. It's too easy for the husband to drive his wife out of her mind: he can torment her and no one will ever believe it. Anna couldn't recall how the argument had ended. She had an image of her mother sitting in the kitchen, holding her head in her heads. When she came close, her mother said, "Don't come near me. I don't want *you* anywhere near me." But Anna couldn't remember if it happened after this argument, or some other time.

Anna did remember there had been many, many arguments. She remembered the silence after her father had gone. But no one ever spoke to her about her father leaving. After the night of her dream, he was simply no longer there. She gathered the courage to ask her mother if he was coming back. Her mother said, "No. You made sure of that." That was all she ever said on the matter. She turned cold and silent. Some days she wouldn't even look at Anna. Other days, she stared at her, as if inspecting her for signs of something, Anna didn't know what.

For months afterwards, Anna wrote letters to her father, apologising for everything she must have done to drive him away, and promising to be better. She would try to be pretty, she promised to grow up beautiful, she swore she would, even though there were no signs of this being likely. She wrote letters to her mother, too, but ripped them up and threw them in the fire. Anna was sure her father would eventually forgive her and come home. When he didn't, she began to wonder if he had ever been there in the first place. Her memories of him were so few, and now so polluted by her dream images, she realised she had come to think of him as a fiction. Someone she had made up. No more or less real than a character in a film.

II

Anna stopped the film before the credits and rewound it. While it was rewinding, she went into the kitchen to pour herself a glass of wine. She opened the kitchen cupboard and took out a glass. She dropped it on the floor. Was it an accident? Let's say it was. But then she took out another glass and dropped that one, too. Deliberately. She liked it and she didn't want to stop. She dropped the glasses on the floor, one after the other, smashing every one to smithereens. She cut her foot, watched a ball of blood roll down between her toes. She stood for a long time, barefoot in the broken glass, and the thought occurred to her that she should be filming this. It would make an excellent piece of film. Maybe she should cut up her mother's film and make something new out of it. Some kind of installation, a new narrative to make sense of the disjointed, disconnected scenes of her childhood.

It was satisfying to break all those glasses, and to know that whatever happened, they could never be put back together again. The glasses had ceased to exist. They were something else now. But she wasn't sure how she would move from the spot in the kitchen. The floor was covered in broken glass, sheer shards of fine crystal, shattered over the tiles. She would cut her feet badly if she tried to step out of there. She'd have to pick out a path, carefully. Perhaps she ought to telephone someone to come and help.

In the other room, the film stopped rewinding and Anna heard it whirr and click and begin to play again. Soft strains of music floated through to the kitchen. It was strange that it started playing by itself. She couldn't remember if that's what videotapes always did. She was thinking about it when she heard footsteps in the hallway.

He was walking slowly, his shoes clicking against the old terracotta tiles. Anna could hear the scrape and wish of his palms running over the wallpaper.

"Is someone there," she said, but the words were choked and strangled in her throat. There was no answer, only the sound of his skin brushing against the walls.

Anna grabbed a large slice of broken glass, held it in her fist like a weapon, cutting her own palm on its edge. There couldn't be anyone in her house. If someone had broken in, she would kill them and no one could blame her. It was self-defence. She heard him stepping into the kitchen, crunching glass under his shoes. She couldn't help it: she closed her eyes.

She didn't believe in ghosts. But she could smell him: trash and blood. She could hear the rustle of his wings.

II

In the darkness that followed, Anna broke open a pearl of memory. It was a hard stone, lodged in her throat for more than fifty years. It stopped her from eating, from laughing, from speaking. It was a tiny thing she'd kept hidden from herself, inside herself. And now she coughed it up, shining with blood, and caught it in her fist. It was so small. But it was like splitting the atom. Such a tiny thing. What a big surprise inside.

She huddled under the bed covers, her knees pulled up to her chin. The dream had been terrible, but worse now: her father was outside the bedroom door, knocking gently. *Little heart, little heart*, he called out. He sounded like himself, but Anna had seen him in his mask of feathers and bones. She knew when he entered the room that he would smell strange and look strange. And whatever he'd done to

Anna's mother, he would do to Anna. He always said he loved her more, despite her ugliness. He always said she was his little heart.

"Come out," he called from the other side of the door. "Do as you're told, child."

Then there was silence, a long empty silence. Anna wasn't sure if he'd gone away. She crept out of bed, silently, and tiptoed to the door. Pressing her ear to the wood, she heard the haunting sounds of music. Carefully, she opened the door. Her father was gone. But the music was a little louder and clearer out on the landing. It was coming from downstairs.

The house was completely dark. She was the lightest thing in it, in her little white nightdress. She tiptoed down the stairs, following the sound of the music. It came from behind the cellar door. Anna wanted to hear the music more: it was beautiful and enchanting, like the sound of a playground or a fair. There was laughter in the music, and children's voices. Anna opened the cellar door and the music swelled up. She switched on the light. It was a bare bulb hanging over the stairs, too dim to illuminate much, but Anna could see wet moss on the stone steps, and water lapping below. She picked her way down the stairs, and when she reached the water's edge, she stepped in, and the music rose up and swallowed her. It washed her up on a dark sand beach, at the top of which was her house. Identical in every way, but very much in the wrong place. So it must be a dream, Anna decided. It's just a dream that feels real, or something real that feels like a dream. Don't be afraid. The music was loud and insistent now. It drew her to her feet and as she stood, he flew close to her, his wings spread out and his beak pushing towards her. *Won't you join the dance*, he said, with his voice like dirt. He enfolded her in the humid embrace of his wings. She couldn't stop him, she was too small to stop him. Besides, she loved him. He tore against her flesh, his beak sliced open her thigh, cutting through the meat right down to the white. Pink and tender flesh clung to the raw bone. He was only celluloid and ink. He was only a memory, a dream of her father. But he was teeming with dead girls under his wings, he had pinned their hair and eyes and tongues to his feathers. He called them all *little heart* as he dug his beak into their soft fleshes.

If it were a dream, she would wake up now. Now. Now!

He was lost in his reverie of feeding. He bent his neck to suck up her blood, and she saw the opportunity of his bare skin under the feathers, skin that was thin and fragile. The slice of glass went in easily, gently to that soft spot. He groaned and spurted blood over her hands and face.

Anna felt the moment coalesce in her hands. She felt the moment when he ceased to exist, and the broken thing came into existence. At the moment of breakage, her father was graphically reduced to his core: a broken, bloodied, ugly, feathered thing, a little heart that spewed blood until it finally ran dry. She watched him fold into himself like black-winged origami and disappear.

Ⅱ

Now.

In the precise moment of breakage, Anna experienced beauty. She experienced it as a child, breaking her father's heart. She relived it now, as herself, bursting open to the knowledge of herself, tearing down the trash-winged ugly celluloid shape of her father, slicing the film into thousands of plasticky pieces. Her own beauty erupted from her hands, struck like lightning, rained broken glass on the floor. A bright glitter of rain, crashing against the stone. It was a big surprise to see all that beauty. She wished she had known it was there inside her all along, waiting for its moment to live.

Virtually Famous

Phil Sloman

He'd died a thousand times today and would die a thousand more, remembering little to nothing of what had passed previously. Each time he felt nothing and would continue to do so ad infinitum. He'd been chosen because of his fame and his looks. A chiselled jawline shadowed with the appropriate thickness of stubble. Blonde hair which defied the laws of gravity and held just so. And those piercing blue eyes which looked as if they had been crafted by the Devil himself. He wasn't perfect. He had habits. Ones frowned upon in polite society. Habits he kept hidden as best he could. The producers who had come calling didn't care about any of that other than to consider the media coverage his involvement would evoke. After all, a history of drink and drugs was to be expected as were his rotational visits to rehab—a place it was suggested he would have a permanent room in one day.

From a young age, he became used to seeing his image wherever he went. It was inescapable. His smile lit up billboards across America when he was barely nine and he had been in and out of the magazines ever since he could remember. He grew up in front of the American public, going from baby-faced sweetheart to teenage heartthrob only to fall from grace before them too. And he fell hard. Harder than he thought was possible. He had regular fights with his parents in his late teens. The arguments were mainly over the money he was making for them and how little came his way. The tabloids lapped it up. The eventual 'divorce' from his parents was splashed across the front of every tittle-tattle rag and website in the country. That was the event which most commentators speculated to be the true catalyst for his subsequent problems. Directors stopped working with him in the years which followed as a chaotic reputation blossomed around him. He was reduced to walk-on parts on cable comedy shows or taking roles in low budget straight-to-DVD films. Invariably these ended up in the $1 bins within weeks of their release. Yet in the early part of his twenties he experienced a brief renaissance in his fortunes. A surprise hit science fiction movie revived interest in his career. This was followed by a spate of supporting roles in more high profile productions, with rumours abound he was in line for the next big blockbuster, only for his addictions to drag him down into the gutter once more. He was all but washed up for a second time before he'd even made it to his thirties.

It was no wonder he took the job when he received the call.

Ⅱ

"Chet Tyler?"

Chet looked up from his magazine. The publication was a glossy affair which purported to expose the salacious truth of the celebrity world. It landed clumsily on the coffee table in the middle of the waiting room as he flung it to one side. Rising, he uncurled his body from the depths of his seat, a modern design full of impractical curves and soft cushioning. Other men sat in similar chairs, each of them struggling to hold on to their twenties. They were all of a type, a selection of clones, the sort

203

which caused heads to turn and cameras to flash. If you squinted it became impossible to readily discern one from the other. Greens and reds played across their perfect cheekbones and blemish-free foreheads, flickering light spilling from flat screen monitors inserted into the surrounding walls. The *Transgressive Games* logo flashed up on each screen simultaneously as it had done on repeat for the thirty minutes Chet had been waiting. Images of people laughing and having fun followed the logo, folks drinking champagne and partying into the night, all shown through the eyes of an anonymous host. Chet ignored all of this and opened the narrow door to the subsequent room.

The room was almost barren, the walls white and devoid of decoration. Towards the rear was a desk of a style commonplace in the receptions of large corporate organisations. A woman sat positioned behind the desk, staring intently at the screen in front of her. A small headset was fixed over a bobbed haircut, the thin stem of the mouthpiece tight against her right cheek. Her lips moved as she engaged in conversation. Every now and then she tapped a manicured fingernail at the screen as if reassuring herself of the evidence of her argument.

Chet coughed.

The woman paused in her conversation, raising an eyebrow as she looked in his direction, her hand covering her mouthpiece.

"I heard my name over the speakers," he ventured, locking and unlocking his fingers, unsure of what to do with his hands as he stood waiting.

"Through there." Her extended arm indicated a secondary door to his right which he had not previously noticed. "He'll be waiting for you in there."

He went to ask her why she hadn't told him that when he stepped into the room. It was clear why he was there. And, after all, didn't she know who he was? Instead he said "Sure," and followed her direction.

Her conversation continued as the door shut behind him.

"Chet! How are you, buddy?" The accent was thick New Yorker. Chet's hand was pumped vigorously in a grip formed of sausage fingers draped with gold, his smaller hand dwarfed between two clam shells.

"Fine, I guess," said Chet. He looked down at the hands holding his. There was something he needed to remember about them. Something he couldn't quite recall.

"You sure? You don't look so great."

"Yeah, I'm good. I'm good." His voice belied his certainty. Chet glanced up from the hands and back at the man who had greeted him, taking in the room at the same time.

It was the size of a school gymnasium. The walls were painted black and led up to an innocuous ceiling set high above the ground. There was an absence of natural daylight throughout; each and every window was covered with dark heavy cloth. Illumination for the room bled down from mounted strip lighting positioned at regular intervals along the ceiling. A few chairs were scattered here and there across the floor, most of them standing upright. A cloth covered table was set up on the far side of the room with an array of paraphernalia decked out along its surface. Beyond that was a room within a room. A rectangle formed of weighted curtains hanging from a prefabricated shell. Oversized spotlights faced into the space like miniature suns burning brightly in the dark. A single video camera stood staring into the canvass screened room, mounted on a tripod and abandoned for now.

"Was it the wait? I guess it was the wait." A meaty hand slapped him on the back in apology. "Sorry, Chet, I had a few things to sort out in here."

"Are you seeing others today? I thought I was the only one."

"Others?"

"In the waiting area. The others there."

Chet's host dropped his smile momentarily, putting a hand to his face. He stroked his jawline as he studied Chet's features before reaching across and patting him on the shoulder.

"Don't worry about them, Chet. This is all about you." The hand dropped down Chet's arm and Chet felt a gentle tug on his elbow. "Let's go, shall we?"

Chet allowed himself to be guided, shuffling one foot in front of the other like a somnambulist. There was a familiarity to the building he couldn't ascribe. Perhaps it was the mundaneness of the interior, the sparsity of detail confusing it with a multitude of other studios he had been inside. He simply couldn't tell why but he knew it was important.

The items on the trestle table were more apparent as they ventured closer toward the camera. They reminded Chet of props he had used on a short lived gangster serial. He had been the hero, a smart-mouthed cop who invariably blurred the lines between legality and anarchy. Only three episodes had aired before the network pulled the plug. He didn't care. He had blown his money from the show on a month long ingestion of amphetamines and alcohol as he partied with a medley of people whose faces he could not remember.

"Have I been here before?" he asked.

His guide turned to look Chet in the face.

"You don't remember?"

Chet remained silent, taking in the barren architecture.

"You once told me this is where The Game was born," his host continued. "This was where it all began. Out here in the middle of nowhere."

"The Game?" queried Chet, rolling the words over his tongue, testing the power of the syllables out loud. "The Game?"

"Yes, Chet. The motherfucking Game." The man opposite sighed. His face loomed closer to Chet's, peering inquisitively into his eyes. "Jeez, how much stuff did you take this time?"

"This time?" Chet took a step back, creating distance between the pair of them, his eyes refocusing on the rotund face which seemed so full of queries.

"Don't worry about it, kid." Those sausage fingers again, this time patting his cheek, leaving a sheen of grease on Chet's face. "Let's get on with this, shall we?"

II

The Game.

It had been a smash hit. A billion dollar success. Sold out in all territories across the globe. People could not get enough. Employees found themselves fired from their jobs whilst lost within The Game. Rumours abounded that people had even died during gameplay from malnutrition, something the media had been happy to hype. And the developers milked it for everything it was worth. The more warnings they slapped on The Game the more people wanted to buy it. Within the first year it was estimated over sixty-five percent of the US population had played The Game at one time or another. And Chet was the face of it. His journey back to stardom was complete.

The rise of virtual reality and the public's obsession with celebrity and riches had created the perfect storm. The Game captured the zeitgeist, riding the wave of desire and jealousy with consummate ease. It dragged the fame-hungry into a world of luxury and decadence, things most had only been able to dream of before. Of course it hadn't been called The Game in its infancy. Back then it had carried Chet's name but that had changed as The Game evolved. Chet's World had been a place for people to be Chet. It was their chance to escape into celebrity culture in a way the magazines, reality shows and PR-operated social media accounts could never hope to match. Within seconds of jacking into The Game you were Chet. Living and breathing his life. A synthesised existence updated with new storylines every single day. The coding was exquisite. The experience sublime. Everything was based on Chet's life, all of it filmed twenty-four hours previously over a morning or afternoon before being uploaded to the system. An integrated artificial intelligence filled in the rest, developing multiple outcomes based on the real life footage. A million variations all from one common source. Reality blurred with fiction. Truth became meaningless. Interpretation redundant. Experience everything.

Over time Chet's World changed, morphing into something unexpected, becoming something new with one simple edict. One which appealed to the base nature of its fandom. One attuned to the seething cocktail of envy and aggression. One which had the

208

simplest of resolutions. The Game became how to kill Chet Tyler.

No one was ever truly able to pinpoint the moment of transition. Theories were rife among social commentators, vloggers and technology experts. Some suggested rogue hackers had engineered a backdoor into the system. Others hypothesised this had always been the end game for the developers, a way to create an addiction and then feed the public with more hardcore storylines as their need for a stronger fix grew. The most common conjecture described a scenario where the system's artificial intelligence had simply responded to the needs of the audience.

Chet's World, or The Game as it became, had always allowed people to play as any number of characters. Friends could jack in as part of a multi-player package, appearing as members of Chet's entourage or as random fans desperate to get his autograph and maybe something a little more salacious.

However, in the beginning it was only the minority who played this way. The majority wanted to be Chet and experience fame first hand, to sip from the Devil's cup so to speak. A not insubstantial number of players ended up in therapy convinced they were Chet Tyler after being submersed in The Game for far too long.

What no one knew until much later was that the only person who knew exactly what it was like to be Chet Tyler was a player of The Game too.

At first Chet had watched remotely. There were any amount of internet channels where he could view gamers waxing lyrical about their online actions as they simulcast their immersion in The Game. It had been a novelty initially. An amusing way to pass time between shoots. A half hour here or an hour snatched there. His viewing time increased as the months wore on. Mild vanity gradually turned to addiction without his realising, even as Chet's World evolved. The first time he saw himself die he was lying in his own bed, silk sheets covering his legs and groin, his chest exposed to the world. He was halfway between sleep and consciousness with only his own narcissism keeping his eyes from closing. The onscreen point of view had been that of a fan's as they approached him at a signing for his autobiography; ghostwritten by a writer he had only ever spoken to by phone. Chet never saw the gun which shot him. The weapon was off-camera, held too low, and fired from the shooter's hip. All he saw was the reaction on his face as the bullet bit deep into his chest followed by a flower of crimson spreading across the white landscape of his immaculately presented shirt. Chet's hands had instinctively clutched to his chest in real life, grasping at the spot inches beneath his clavicle where the bullet had entered his virtual body. He had watched himself die in films a hundred times before but this was different. This time his death was more personal, more grounded in reality. Chet swallowed desperate gulps of air as his brain struggled to process the images on screen. His fingers went from his chest to the covers, his body forming a crucifix as he grasped for purchase as his whole world collapsed around him. It was only when the adrenaline kicked in that he was able to regain composure. After that it became a new addiction for him. Another hit for an old time junkie. He sought out the videos of his online demise. The darker the better. There was an elaborateness in some of his deaths which continued to surprise him over and over again. The only limit was the imagination of the gamer. Sometimes people took it to a whole new level, torturing him for hours

210

on end before either his body gave out or the perpetrator's own levels of boredom prompted them to resolve the situation. And all the time the download figures for the clips continued climbing up and up and up.

He remembered the faces of all those who'd killed him in The Game: a red-faced double-chinned man in a navy business suit; another heavily bearded, with a distinctive port-red birth mark on his face. A nurse, two women who looked like sisters. A blank-faced man with a bald head getting out from behind the wheel of a taxi with a gun in his hand; a woman in a long black nightdress stepping from a hotel room wielding silver scissors, her bare feet bloodied. Even a young girl, once, a thin broomstick of a thing, bruised knees and grubby palms.

He remembered their faces from The Game. At least, that's where he hoped he remembered them from.

II

Chet and his host approached the video camera within the curtained area. One foot placed after another, after another, after another, the sound of their footsteps hollow in the vastness of the room. Chet stopped. He could feel a tackiness clutching at the soles of his sneakers. He imagined warm gum on the sidewalk softened by the heat of the midday sun but the pull was subtler than that. He looked to his feet. The outline of an irregular patch of darkness was partially visible against the black texture of the flooring. Other footsteps had corrupted the mark and overlaid it with dirt from the soles of their shoes. Chet crouched down. He dragged his finger along the ground feeling a mixture of grit and something which

211

resembled semi-dried syrup. Strawberry perhaps. He lifted his finger to see what it was.

Chet paused. His companion was standing by the curtains. His portly physique silhouetted in the blaze of light behind him as if in homage to Hitchcock on those old TV shows Chet's dad made him watch as a kid. Hitchcock was shouting words at Chet. Trying to get his attention.

"Chet. I need you here, Chet. I need to know if this was you. I really need to know if this was you."

II

"Would it be murder or suicide?" It was a question he asked himself innumerable times before he finally took the plunge.

There had been failed attempts where he geared himself up for the deed only to relent at the last minute. He likened it in his mind to inserting a needle into your own veins. The fear of the pain was always greater than the reality. One moment of discomfort followed by hours of reward and ecstasy.

He had chosen pills in the end. Ground up and mixed with a cocktail of Jägermeister, schnapps and honey liqueur to disguise the taste. It was meant to be a kindness. A way for faux-Chet to drift off into the electronic nether with the minimal of pain. It was the way he would want to go himself when the time came. He had not anticipated the vomiting and the pleading. Slender fingers had grasped at his avatar's trouser leg, gripping the fabric for dear life. Chet had watched his own face staring up at him imploringly, begging for help, blood flecked saliva foaming on lips he had used for the most intimate of pastimes. Hands belonging to his character pushed faux-Chet away, leaving the virtual him to whimper on the floor in a nauseating pool of its own stomach fluids. Five minutes of listening to the agonised mewling had been enough. He had acted without thinking. Grabbing the nearest thing to hand. Repeatedly bludgeoning the bottle of spirits into faux-Chet's skull. Over and over and over again. Playing a perverse game of whack-a-mole with only one target and with the strokes meeting less resistance as the pulpy mass on the floor increased.

It was a month before he tried again. This time he used a gun. He assumed the role of one of his entourage to get close to faux-Chet, taking the shot from behind. The nose of the gun had nestled into faux-Chet's thick blonde hair, singeing the locks with the flare from the muzzle. This way he didn't have to look himself in the eyes as he did it. This way he could remind himself it was all still part of a game. A harmless, non-deadly game. By the end of that week he had killed himself twenty-seven more times.

He experimented. He took inspiration from the videos posted by other gamers. People he regarded as artists pushing boundaries. He found new weapons of choice. After all, he had nothing but time on his hands. By now he was a recluse. He had quit the pre-recording shoots which fed the system. The developers hadn't cared. It saved them an unnecessary overhead leaving the gameplay to be completely generated by the inbuilt AI. Chet had cited the risks to his wellbeing of filming any more scenes and that, in part, had been true. It had become too dangerous for Chet to live his normal life, whatever normal meant in that context. Stalkers had increased dramatically in tangent with the rise in sales of The Game. So he simply stayed in his room watching videos and jacking into The Game while spending a fortune on deliveries and home security. It was when the cutting started that things became worse.

II

Chet stood up.

"Chet, I need to know if this was you."

Chet licked his finger absentmindedly, ignoring the rasp of grit on his tongue. Whatever it was, it didn't taste like strawberry syrup. He ignored the pull at his sneakers as he walked to the curtained area.

"Chet, are you with me, buddy?" Two finger clicks sounded off in front of his face. "Chet, I need to know if you're in the room."

Chet blinked twice. His nostrils flared, inhaling deeply as he took in the scene.

"This wasn't me," he muttered, throwing his hands up to the sides of his temples. "This wasn't me."

He stumbled backwards, rushing from the curtained area, his legs rotating unnaturally beneath him as he lost his balance. He fell partly on the floor and partly into the props table, his head connecting with the cloth-covered edge. His fingers grasped at the cheap fabric, pulling it down level with him as he tried to claw his way to standing. Scalpels, gougers, chisels, hammers and blades of varying lengths clattered on the surrounding ground. A knife missed his splayed fingers as it fell point first to the floor. It stood upright with the tip held fast. Chet looked at the fallen blade with part of it reflecting the artificial light and the other part coated with a substance he knew did not taste of strawberry syrup.

II

"Which one is me? Which one is me? Which one is me?"

It was a mantra Chet rocked himself to sleep with, his arms wrapped around his knees as he sat up in bed.

"Which one is me? Which one is me? Which one is me?"

The repetition was soothing, muttered with the insistent rhythm of a commuter train at full throttle.

"Which one is me? Which one is me? Which one is me?"

Exhaustion would claim him eventually. It always did.

His dreams were the same as his new reality, the one he lived online. In them he would be watching Chet Tyler but he was never sure if it was faux-Chet or himself. He had a scalpel in his dreams, a small one the same as the clinicians used in the cosmetic surgeries dotted across the Hollywood hills. Chet or faux-Chet or whoever the fuck it was would always be compliant, sitting in a docile manner staring into the nothingness of the world, waiting for the inevitable to happen. There was a nonchalant swagger as he approached, scalpel in hand, a smile on his face, at ease with the inevitability of what was about to happen. He would sit astride their lap and pretend he was looking into the mirror as the cutting began, his muscles knotting and relaxing as he fought to keep the visage intact while the knife cut away the connecting tissue. He needed to see what lay beneath the façade. He needed to know if the real Chet was in there or if the real Chet was really still him.

He woke early with the deaths from his dreams echoing inside his head. A xylophone of ribs stood prominent beneath his skin as he sat naked on the oversized bed. The jack slid easily into his neck, the sensation familiar and reassuring like slipping into conversation with an old friend. It took less than a second for him to be ported into his other reality. The welcome point blinked into view as the system took over his neural indicators.

"Good morning," the system announced. Chet watched the woman seated behind the desk as she spoke. "Who would you like to be today?"

"Vinny. I'd like to be Vinny today."

"Of course. Please go through there. They'll be expecting you."

His fingers locked and unlocked as he stood waiting. An effervescent tingle passed momentarily from his scalp down to his toes. The experience was always the same as the AI adjusted the player's avatar. He knew what he would see if he looked in a mirror. He had worn this person so many times before. Killed himself a hundred times from inside this body. He'd see the chubby hands. The gold jewellery. The slight role of neck flab. The receding hairline hovering above a thin slick of sweat. A perfect simulation of Chet's manager.

Chet stepped through the door on the far side of the room.

♊

"Chet, you need to answer me. This one is too close to home."

Chet looked from the knife to Vinny.

Vinny wearily ran a hand across his face. He exhaled in a controlled manner, long and slow, scrunching his eyes shut as he pinched the bridge of

216

his nose. He let his hand drop and spoke to Chet as if he were a parent talking to a child.

"Chet, it's the meds. I know it's the meds. Everything's going to be fine." He edged two steps towards his client with hands raised in what he hoped would be a placating manner.

"Stay away from me, Vinny. I'm warning you."

Vinny checked his progress. Chet was moving, using the upturned table for purchase to enable him to stand. The knife was no longer visible on the floor.

"Chet? What are you doing, Chet?"

Chet's legs quivered as he steadied his stance. The knife was in plain sight now, held firmly out in front of him.

"Don't mess with me, Chet. Not now. Not today. We've a small window of opportunity to make this go away but I need the truth."

"I'm not the one who is lying!"

"Listen, if it wasn't for me you would be sitting in a cell right this fucking minute."

"You're lying!"

"I followed you, Chet. I came all the way out here to the middle of nowhere just to make sure you were fine. And this was what I found." Vinny spread his arms wide, indicating the curtained scene behind him. "Chet, there's a man's body lying in there with its goddamned motherfucking face cut off! Now I need you to tell me if that was you and then I can deal with it."

"Of course it wasn't me!"

"Then who was it! You got in a car, the pair of you, and drove out here. Jeez, did you film it, Chet? Is that what the camera's for?"

"Drove with who?"

217

"You and your latest beau. Harold was it?" Vinny snorted a laugh. "I bet you didn't even know his name."

"I don't know anyone called..." Chet stopped. "Wait. Wait. They'll tell you."

"Who, Chet? Who will tell me?"

"The lady in the reception, the others in the waiting room. They'll tell you I've been waiting here for ages. I couldn't have done it."

A look of pity crossed Vinny's face.

"There is no reception, Chet. Just this hangar of a studio. If you don't believe me go see for yourself. Go on. The door's right there."

Chet's eyes followed the direction Vinny was pointing in, back to where he had entered the room.

"I found you passed out in the corner when I got here, Chet."

Chet ignored him and strode for the exit.

"You were lying right over there."

The door was feet away. Five steps and he would be there.

Four.

Three.

"Don't go through there, Chet. You don't want to go through that door." Vinny's voice rose louder the further Chet got from him. "You won't like what you see."

Two.

"Chet!"

One.

Chet's hand grasped the handle and the door swung open.

"I told you, Chet. I warned you. You wouldn't listen to me."

Chet clutched at the jamb of the door with his free hand, looking out into the sandy terrain spread out before him. Two cars sat parked outside.

"I don't understand. They were there. There was a room…and a desk…and a woman. They were real."

Vinny's footsteps sounded behind him, coming closer.

"The others in the waiting room, they were watching the screens. There was a reality show playing. No wait. It was a game. A game was playing."

"There was no room, Chet. There was no game."

Chet started to chuckle, letting the knife hang limp in his grip.

"What are you laughing at, Chet? I don't get it. What's so goddamned funny?"

"I remember. I remember now. You said it when I got here. This is where The Game started. We're in The Game." Chet's eyes sparkled with withheld tears. "All this time we've been in The Game."

"There is no Game, Chet. You're the one who always told me about The Game. You made it up. Try to remember, Chet. It's the meds messing with your head. Making up things which don't exist. Don't you remember anything?"

"We're in The Game, Vinny." Chet's words were more assured. "That's it, Vinny. You're just a collection of pixels. It's as simple as that. All I have to say is two words."

"Don't do it, Chet."

"You can't stop me. Don't you get it, no one can stop me."

"Chet, I'm warning you. You don't want to do it."

"Game over, game over," shouted Chet, arms spread as if performing to a crowd.

Vinny waited, watching.

"Game over."

Nothing changed.

Chet looked inside and outside the room, spinning in a circle, looking for an exit point to reality.

"I said 'Game over'!"

"Shouting's not going to change anything, Chet."

Chet dropped to his knees, clawing at the back of his neck as he hit the floor, grasping for the jack point which existed in real life.

"I tried to tell you, kid. It was all in your head. The doctors confirmed it. You must remember that."

Vinny crouched beside Chet, sighing gently as he took the bulk of his weight on his knees. He put a paternal hand on Chet's brow. Spittle and air bubbles formed on Chet's lips as he repeated his failed litany in an attempt to exit the system.

"This is what happened, Chet." Vinny's words were quiet and calm. "You lured Harold here with promises of who knows what. Maybe you were going to make him famous or maybe it was sex and drugs. Either way, that's his blood on the floor. That's his corpse inside the curtains with his pretty young face on the ground beside him."

"That's not true," spluttered Chet.

Vinny ignored him.

"You took that knife in your hand and used it on him. You had to know what was underneath. Whether it was you or not. It's not the first time, Chet. That's why the doctors had you on the meds. But it's got to stop now. It can't continue any more."

"Bullshit, Vinny. Bullshit. It was you. It's always you."

220

Tears were streaming down Chet's cheeks, his words slurred between a mixture of snot and confusion.

"Now, Chet, we both know that's not true."

"It is true. It was you."

Vinny stroked Chet's hair, calming an upset child. His right hand disappeared into his jacket pocket feeling for the reassuring weight of the gun inside.

"Don't worry, Chet. It will soon be alright. Uncle Vinny is going to make this go away just like he always does."

Ⅱ

The woman sat behind the desk revealing perfect teeth within a perfect smile. The smile never faltered as the man entered the room. He was in his late twenties sporting a face which caused heads to turn and cameras to flash.

He stood waiting patiently for her to speak, his hands held together, his fingers locking and unlocking with a mild sense of anticipation, ready for what was to come.

"Good morning," she said. "Who would you like to be today?"

The Imposters

Gary McMahon

Gary McMahon is the author of many novels, novellas and story collections. His short fiction has been reprinted in several Year's Best anthologies. He lives and works in West Yorkshire, where aside from writing his interests are karate, cycling and cinema. Gary has a doppelgänger who goes around in a flowery shirt being nice to people. He knows he does. And when Gary finds him, things will get messy.

Laura Mauro

Laura Mauro is a London-born, Essex-based laboratory technician moonlighting as a writer of strange stories. Her work has previously appeared in *Black Static*, *Shadows and Tall Trees* and various anthologies, and in 2015 she was nominated for a British Fantasy Award, which was quite nice. In her spare time she collects cats, acquires tattoos, and dyes her hair strange colours. She has a twin brother, and if she had to make a guess she'd say she is probably the changeling.

Timothy J Jarvis

Timothy J. Jarvis is a writer and scholar with an interest in the antic, the weird, the strange. His first novel, *The Wanderer*, was published by Perfect Edge Books in the summer of 2014. His short-fiction has appeared in *Murder Ballads*, *Booklore*, *Uncertainties: Volume I*, *Caledonia Dreamin': Strange Fiction of Scottish Descent*, *3:AM Magazine*, and *Leviathan 4: Cities*, among other places. He is also interested in drone and ambient music and has collaborated with sound artists on sleeve notes and performance.

Holly Ice

Holly Ice loves the unusual, and subjects which bring out a numinous longing for more than reality can provide. She writes in the horror, sci-fi and fantasy genres and has always hoped to one day stumble across a magical world, hidden from modern society. Knowing that may well be unlikely, her first goal is to convince her boyfriend to adopt a cat.

Neil Williamson

Neil Williamson's latest book, *The Memoirist*, is a near-future SF novella about living in a deeply pervasive surveillance society. His other books include *The Moon King*, *Secret Language* and *The Ephemera*. He lives, writes and makes music in Glasgow.

Stephen Bacon

Stephen Bacon's fiction has been published in *Black Static*, *Shadow & Tall Trees*, *Cemetery Dance*, *Postscripts*, and many other magazines and anthologies. Several of his stories have been selected for *Best Horror of the Year*. He is the author of the novellas *Lantern Rock*, *Laudanum Nights* and *Cockatrice*. He lives in South Yorkshire with his wife and two sons.

Ralph Robert Moore

Ralph Robert Moore's fiction has appeared in a wide variety of genre and literary magazines and anthologies. His books include the novels *Father Figure*, *As Dead As Me*, and *Ghosters*, and the story collections *Remove the Eyes*, *I Smell Blood*, and *You Can Never Spit It All Out*. He has been nominated twice for Best Story of the Year by The British Fantasy Society, and is a columnist with Black Static magazine. His website SENTENCE is at www.ralphrobertmoore.com.

Tracy Fahey

Tracy Fahey is a Gothic fiction writer. In 2017, her debut collection *The Unheimlich Manoeuvre* was shortlisted for a British Fantasy Award. Two of her short stories, 'Walking The Borderlines' and 'Under The Whitethorn' were long listed for Honourable Mentions in *The Best Horror of the Year Volume 8*. She is published in fifteen US and UK anthologies. Her website is www.tracyfahey.com.

Georgina Bruce

Georgina Bruce writes weird fiction which can be found in *Interzone, Black Static,* and various other magazines and anthologies. Her short story 'White Rabbit' is nominated for a British Fantasy Society award. She tweets as @monster_soup.

Phil Sloman

Phil Sloman is a writer of dark fiction and was nominated for a BFA Best Newcomer award for his novella *Becoming David* released by Hersham Horror in 2016.

Phil likes to peak behind the curtain of reality and see what might be lurking there. Sometimes he writes down what he sees. He hails from the south coast of England and has written numerous short stories which can be found throughout various anthologies. In the humdrum of everyday life, Phil lives with an understanding wife and a trio of vagrant cats who tolerate their human slaves. There are no bodies buried beneath the patio as far as he is aware. Occasionally Phil can be found lurking here: http://insearchofperdition.blogspot.co.uk/ or wasting time on Facebook—come say hi.

James Everington

James Everington checked into a room in *The Hyde Hotel* with Dan Howarth in 2016. Whether what checked out was him, a clone, double, or pod-person is unclear.

But he/it has since released *The Quarantined City* from Infinity Plus (which *The Guardian* quite liked) as well as the novella *Paupers' Graves.* James - or his double - is still updating his website https://jameseverington.blogspot.co.uk so you can seek further clues to his identity there.

Dan Howarth

Dan Howarth is a Mancunian born writer who is now living on Merseyside and experiencing horror first hand. Like all Northerners he enjoys beer, rain and stories of the occult. His fiction can be found online, in sporadic physical publications including *No Monsters Allowed* (edited by Alex Davis) and scrawled in blood on the walls of a nearby underpass.

♊

83923146R00124

Made in the USA
Columbia, SC
14 December 2017